Bolan reached into the car and dragged out the dealer

"Start walking." He gave Pablo Obregon a shove and fell in step one pace behind him, using the man as a shield as they headed toward Francisco and the exchange.

"That's far enough," the Executioner warned.

"I have the woman, as you can see," the drug lord called. "She's getting wet. Perhaps if we make haste—"

The sound of automatic-weapons fire exploded from the greenery behind Bolan's adversaries, bullets whispering across the rain-swept parking lot. From the expression on Francisco's face, and the way he ducked to save himself and dragged Alicia with him, it was apparent that his men weren't responsible.

Pablo bolted, racing toward the cover of his brother's limo. Bolan dodged back toward his rental, reached inside and freed the parking brake. As the car rolled forward, he raised the Colt Commando to his shoulder and triggered the 40 mm buckshot round.

If the Executioner had to die this day, he'd make damn sure that he wouldn't die alone.

D0972818

MACK BOLAN ®

The Executioner

DON PENDLETON'S
THE EXECUTIONER®
DEADLY CONTEST

A GOLD EAGLE BOOK FROM

WORLDWIDE®

TORONTO • NEW YORK • LONDON
AMSTERDAM • PARIS • SYDNEY • HAMBURG
STOCKHOLM • ATHENS • TOKYO • MILAN
MADRID • WARSAW • BUDAPEST • AUCKLAND

First edition February 1995
ISBN 0-373-61194-3

Special thanks and acknowledgment to
Mike Newton for his contribution to this work.

DEADLY CONTEST

Politics is the hard dealing of hard men over properties; their strength is in dealing with their virility.

—Norman Mailer

Hell has three gates: lust, anger, and greed.

—the *Bhagavad Gita*

Politics and greed make strange bedfellows, they say, and the road to hell is paved with good intentions. If there's any room in hell, I have a few new candidates this time around.

—Mack Bolan

For America's peacekeepers, especially those who have given their lives in Somalia. God keep.

PFC Matthew Anderson
Pvt. Domingo Arroyo, Jr.
Pvt. Anthony Botello
CWO Donovan Briley
S.Sgt. Daniel Busch
Cpl. James Cavaco
Pvt. David Conner
SFC Robert Deeks
SFC Earl Fillmore, Jr.
Pvt. Mark Gutting
Pvt. Daniel Harris
Sgt. Christopher Hilgert
Sgt. James Joyce
Pvt. Richard Kowaleski, Jr.
Pvt. James Martin, Jr.
M.Sgt. Timonth Martin
Spec. Keith Pearson
Spec. Dominick Pila
Sgt. Ferdinan Richardson
Sgt. Ronald Richerson
Pvt. Don Robertson
L.Cpl. William Rose
Sgt. Lorenzo Ruiz
Spec. James Smith
Sgt. Eugene Williams
CWO Clifton Wolcott

PROLOGUE

Mack Bolan smelled the trap before he saw it.

It wasn't a physical aroma, like the smell of rotting meat, but it was palpable to Bolan all the same. Long years of living on the edge in different kinds of jungles had enabled him to sniff the wind and tell if there was something badly out of place.

Like now.

He wasn't standing in the sort of jungle most men recognized. There were no trees, except the decorative kind that had been planted every thirty yards or so to give the urban avenue a gentler, more "natural" atmosphere. The sidewalk underneath his feet was concrete, freshly swept that morning, and the curb was lined with cars.

It was a different kind of jungle with its own endemic predators.

The gray Mercedes made its second pass, heads of its passengers swiveling to cover every angle of attack. Four men, their features indistinct behind the smoky glass, were checking out the street for targets, hazards, anything that might affect their mission.

Bolan could not be entirely certain what that mission was but he was no believer in coincidence. His presence on the street, together with the trolling Mercedes, advised him that the hunters probably had interests similar—if not identical—to his.

And that spelled danger.

The warrior moved along the sidewalk at an easy pace, pretending not to notice the Mercedes as it passed him and headed in the opposite direction. They had made one pass along the street from east to west then reversed the track, as if the driver were confused about an address, searching for the number of a shop, perhaps already late for an appointment. It was absolutely normal in this neighborhood of small boutiques, cafés and hair salons with studio apartments on the upper floors. One group of harried shoppers more or less would draw no comment from the residents or passersby.

Mack Bolan took advantage of the scene in much the same way, dawdling before a window that displayed the latest style in evening wear for men. He watched the luxury vehicle slide by, reflected in the clean plate glass, and waited for the cruising shark to disappear a block downrange.

The warrior had been waiting for the best part of a quarter hour for his contact to appear. It was a blind approach, no prearrangement. He was looking for surprise but that didn't include a hostile welcoming committee with a separate agenda of its own.

The men in the Mercedes hadn't come here in search of Bolan. They were watching out for other prey and logic told him that their target was the same as his. Their purpose though, would be entirely different.

These men would have come to kill.

And Bolan was determined to prevent them from succeeding.

On the far side of the street, reflected in his window mirror, Bolan saw a dark-haired woman suddenly appear. She turned left moving east along the sidewalk with determined strides. From what he saw she didn't seem to give a second glance behind her even though she had to have been aware that there was danger in the city, some of it directed most specifically at her.

He half turned toward the woman, tracking with his eyes, and made a positive ID—dark hair, the chiseled profile, ample curves beneath a stylish two-piece suit. The CIA surveillance photos didn't do her justice but he would have known her anywhere.

And so, the warrior reckoned, would her enemies.

He could have phoned ahead, arranged a meeting in advance, but Bolan was uncertain as to how his overture would be received. If she had cut him off and gone to ground somewhere within the city or outside, then precious time would have been consumed while Bolan tried to reestablish contact.

Wasted time was one thing he couldn't afford. His deadline was already looming and he had no schedule as yet, no concrete plan of action. He was counting on the woman to assist him and to close that deal he felt that it was necessary for the two of them to meet in person. Unexpectedly perhaps, but Bolan thought that he could put her mind at ease once they began to talk.

But now he realized he might not have that chance.

The gray Mercedes was coming back. He glimpsed it from the corner of his eye, eastbound, accelerating as the driver saw his mark and made the move to overtake her on the street. The hunters had another block or so to cover and the vehicle was closing fast.

He slipped the button on his jacket, granting easy access to the autoloading pistol slung beneath his arm. The big Beretta 93-R gave him twenty rounds to play with and the chances were that he would need them all.

He started to walk faster, almost running, trying at the same time not to draw attention from the gunners in the Mercedes. They would be focused on the woman, concentrating on their job. The first two passes had assured them they weren't in danger here.

The warrior came up level with his would-be contact, falling into step with her, the two-lane street between them. On his starboard flank, the Mercedes was gliding closer like a hungry shark in search of prey.

The jerky squeal of brakes told Bolan all he had to know. He ripped the black Beretta from its armpit rig and swiveled, stepping off into the street.

ALICIA GRANDIER KNEW danger very well indeed. Her father's life on New Amsterdam, putting out the news that men of power often wanted to suppress, had taught her all about slashed tires and threatening phone calls in the dead of night, bricks and bottles smashing windows while she slept. Her father had been wounded by a gunman back in 1985 and he still walked with a limp as a result of the attack. It hadn't slowed him to any great degree but there were worry lines around his mouth and eyes. His hair had gone entirely white, though he was only fifty-two years old.

The danger had grown worse of late with the elections coming on. Alicia had opposed her father's run for office but he wouldn't change his mind. The issues in contention were beyond the price of one man's life, he told her, and he had no choice but to proceed at any cost. If he should fall along the way there would be someone else to grasp the torch and carry on.

It frightened her to hear him speak that way because Alicia knew the opposition might be capable of anything. If they could win by guile and bribery, without displays of violence, they would take the path of least resistance. But her father's brisk political campaign was making headway, as reflected in the polls, and every passing day would make his enemies more desperate.

This morning she was off to pay the printer for a brand-new batch of leaflets, after which she would resume her duties at Grandier campaign headquarters downtown. Alicia walked because she liked the exercise and didn't care for driving in the city with congested traffic and the risk of daredevil pedestrians who often seemed intent on suicide.

The countryside was different. Driving up and down the coast or in the mountains northeast of Hollandia, she felt a sense of freedom that was difficult to articulate. She loved to put the top down on her Fiat and let her hair stream in the wind, whipping behind her like an ebony flag.

At the moment she faced another day of answering the telephones, dictating correspondence, making certain that her father's campaign office ran efficiently. She gave no thought to danger in the form of personal attack, although the office was receiving daily threats from callers who predictably refused to state their names. Three times last week, the building had been cleared by bomb threats until they posted guards inside and out to guarantee that no strange faces entered unobserved. Since then, they simply hung up on the nuisance callers, satisfied that empty threats could do no harm.

Alicia took precautions for herself from force of habit, knowing that a number of her father's campaign workers had been threatened and harassed, two of them beaten on separate occasions while putting up posters or handing out campaign literature on the street. Thus far, none of the threats had been directed against her but the potential was there.

She had a can of pepper spray inside her purse but didn't carry any other weapons since her father was a staunch proponent of nonviolence and his teachings had influenced her from childhood. It was better to retreat from danger, she believed, except in cases where a righteous cause demanded that a person face the risk head-on.

This morning though, the last thing on Alicia's mind was any sort of personal attack. The day was bright and clear, not warm enough to make the sidewalks simmer yet, and the radio's prediction of an incoming tropical storm was still in the future, a day or two away with any kind of luck.

Smooth sailing.

The Mercedes came up behind Alicia and on her left, but she was window-shopping, admiring a display of summer dresses. Her first hint of danger was the yelp of rubber on the road as brakes were suddenly applied. She glanced in that direction, and registered a swirl of movement as several men exited a vehicle.

The sudden rush of adrenaline struck home like a fist to the solar plexus. Alicia stepped swiftly back and clutched at her handbag, one hand diving for the can of spray.

She almost made it.

Two men reached her almost simultaneously, one clutching at her left arm while the other took her right, the first man slapping her purse away with contemptuous ease.

Fighting back, Alicia kicked out at the large man on her left, twisting in his grasp and trying to reach the other's face with an elbow. Neither move was terribly effective though she managed to strike a glancing blow to her assailant's shin, eliciting a curse. He slapped her twice across the face, an easy back-and-forth, before a third man joined them, bending easily to grab her ankles out from under her.

Alicia cried out as they hauled her toward the waiting car like so much baggage. Now, belatedly, she lashed her head from side to side in search of witnesses, potential helpers, but her view was blocked by broad shoulders left and right. Another shout and the man on her right reared and slammed a fist into the woman's face.

THE DRIVER SAW Mack Bolan coming, blinked at him in obvious surprise and tapped the horn with one hand as a warning to his friends. The window started down and the muzzle of a shiny automatic pistol followed Bolan, tracking into target acquisition. But the gunner never had a chance to fire.

The powerful Beretta whispered through its custom-made silencer, sending a 9 mm parabellum round toward impact with the driver's nose. His swarthy face imploded, spewing crimson as he slumped back in his seat, deadweight against the springs and stained upholstery. His foot slipped off the clutch and the engine stalled.

One down.

The others were aware of danger but they hadn't pinned it down to a specific source as yet. They were encumbered by the woman; three men with their hands full, when they saw grim death approaching from across the street.

Two of them dropped their burden at once as if on a silent command. Alicia's heels struck the sidewalk with a solid crack, her left side listing toward the ground. She was supported onto on her right now, the third gunner looking frantic, torn between the choice of releasing his captive and helping his comrades defend themselves.

While he was making up his mind, Bolan dealt with the others. The gunner on the left was first, the quicker of the two, losing a button on his jacket as he brought his nickel-plated automatic out of hiding. Bolan put two bullets in his chest from twenty feet away and watched the gunman stagger backward, both arms flailing as he lost his balance and triggered a wide round toward the sky. He hit the sidewalk like a sack of dirty laundry and Bolan dismissed him from mind as he sought a new target.

The second gunner with his hands free at the moment was a slender man, all nose and ears with hair slicked down across a narrow skull. Dark glasses hid his eyes but there was sudden panic in his attitude with two of his companions dead in front of him. His weapon was a "baby" Desert Eagle automatic, chambered for the same 9 mm parabellum cartridge as Bolan's Beretta, and it looked imposing, even in a trembling hand.

The Executioner fired two rounds on the move, one drilling through the gunner's throat and spouting blood across his shirtfront as the second sheared off several inches of his jawline. Reeling, Mr. Shades was on his way to contact with the pavement when a third round made it permanent, exploding through his temple with the solid impact of a hammer stroke.

The last man up had finally decided it was time to save himself at any cost. He dropped Alicia Grandier and Bolan heard a little "Oof!" as she made jarring contact with the sidewalk. The fall seemed to rouse her a bit but Bolan had no time to check on her progress, occupied as he was with the killing at hand.

The last of her captors was heavyset. He wore his pistol in a shoulder rig and fumbled for it with a hand that seemed to lack coordination.

The black Beretta spit a single round, the parabellum mangler's jarring impact rocking Bolan's target backward on his heels. He still kept going for the weapon though, despite aerated blood erupting from a punctured lung and the Executioner put a second round between his eyes to finish it.

Bolan turned toward Alicia Grandier and found her up on hands and knees, shaking her head like a wounded animal. Her nose was bleeding, bright red droplets spattering the pavement between her splayed hands. He moved to her left, crouched beside her, glancing up and down the street to check for other gunmen or coincidental witnesses.

Downrange, a man and woman were emerging from a small café. They saw the Mercedes with three doors standing open, bodies stretched out on the sidewalk.

The warrior wedged the 93-R back into its shoulder rig and slipped one hand beneath the lady's arm, hoisting her to her feet as he rose.

"Come on," he said. "We haven't got much time."

Alicia blinked at him, initially mistaking him for one of her attackers. Then she saw the bodies sprawled around them and something clicked home behind her hazel eyes. She let Bolan lead her from the killing ground across the street and toward the nearby alley where his rental car was waiting with Rafael Encizo at the wheel. Halfway there, a middle-aged shopkeeper got in Bolan's face, risking more than he realized with demands for an explanation, insisting that Bolan and Alicia wait for the police.

The warrior could have killed him where he stood but the man was simply an overweight merchant, albeit casting himself in the role of neighborhood vigilante for a growing audience. Bolan settled the argument with a stiff-fingered jab to the gut that left the man doubled over, gasping at the remnants of his breakfast splattered on his shoes.

Then they were out of there, Encizo gunning it the moment Bolan and Alicia were safely seated in back. Moments later they had merged with traffic on a parallel street, heading west.

A squad car passed them, headed in the opposite direction, lights and siren clearing other vehicles away. Encizo swung over to let it pass, resuming his course once the cruiser had dwindled in his rearview mirror.

They were two miles from the shooting scene when Bolan glanced over and found Alicia Grandier staring at him, a tissue pressed to her nose.

"Who are you?" she asked him, her voice slightly muffled.

"A friend," Bolan answered. "I think I can help."

1

The island of New Amsterdam is shaped like a pork chop with the narrow end aimed northward and its widest point, a swelling toward the east. It measures twenty-seven miles from north to south, eighteen across the midpoint, east to west. A range of thickly wooded mountains form the island's spine and northwest axis. Coffee beans are grown there but despite their excellence, the quantities are relatively small. New Amsterdam earns more from sugarcane, which is farmed on fertile strips of land between the mountains and the coast on east and west.

And there is tourism.

In any given year no fewer than a quarter-million visitors from the United States and Western Europe travel to New Amsterdam. It is estimated that each tourist spends a minimum of fifteen hundred dollars on the island, thereby pumping fresh blood into the economy. Without those tourist dollars, pounds and deutsche marks, many of New Amsterdam's 150,000 year-round residents would starve.

It was not always so. When Dutch explorers found and claimed the island for themselves in 1583, the native "Indians" were more than satisfied with their system of slash-and-burn subsistence agriculture. They were "civilized" by greed and guile, sometimes at gunpoint, but at that, their suffering was less extreme than that of natives toiling under French or Spanish rule on nearby islands, where dismemberment and death were routine forms of "discipline."

Against all odds, the Dutch had held their island colony through wars and revolutions while the European empires dwindled and were broken up into protectorates, republics and the like. By 1948, when natives got the vote by law, most of them truly felt like Dutchmen once removed. A small but vocal independence movement sprang up in the 1960s but it shied away from terrorism and rejected offers of "assistance" from Havana where Castro's fledgling regime was anxious to foster revolution throughout the Western Hemisphere. Most residents of New Amsterdam, in fact, seemed fairly well satisfied with their colonial status. If major wealth was concentrated in the hands of a few well-known families, at least some of them were natives, intermarriages having broken down the color line to some extent, where protests and speeches never would.

But independence was coming, and soon.

At last it was economics, rather than public agitation, that made the Netherlands government anxious to unload one of its four remaining Caribbean possessions. The others—Aruba, Bonaire and Curacao—were close together, easily administered and convenient to the Venezuelan mainland, while New Amsterdam sat by itself some sixty miles due north of Puerto Rico. Administrative costs were climbing all the time and new taxation on the flow of tourist dollars to offset expenses had produced the closest thing to revolution that New Amsterdam had ever seen.

When native merchants rise en masse against a distant government, the rulers must decide if they will fight or walk away. In the case of New Amsterdam, the decision had been made for independence in the interest of economy.

The date was set and the machinery was all in place. Ruud Manders, the elderly governor, was marking time in the last few months of a caretaker administration, waiting for the final vote that would send him back to his native Arnhem. In the meantime he had opted for a laissez-faire approach to governing New Amsterdam, allowing rival parties in the upcoming election to conduct themselves as they saw fit, presumably within the limits of established law. Manders saw no evil on the island but concentrated on his own retirement, long deferred.

But there *was* evil in New Amsterdam, and it had brought the Executioner from southern California on a mission he couldn't refuse.

The story, as explained to him by Hal Brognola back in Washington, was relatively simple. Agents of the DEA had been aware for eighteen months or more that cocaine from Colombia was moving through New Amsterdam en route to Puerto Rico and the States. The traffic was encouraged from Havana where high-ranking members of the Castro regime were said to have substantial interests—both financial and political—in smuggling coke to the United States. The winds of change had toppled Fidel's support system in Russia and Eastern Europe, leaving Havana in pressing need of material assistance from other sources.

What could be more logical than an alliance with the Medellín cartel?

At one stroke, Castro's cronies fattened up the party's coffers, skimmed a profit for themselves and struck a solid blow at the Americans they had reviled since 1959. They watched the U.S. government spend billions for a hopeless "war on drugs" that interdicted less than ten percent of the presumed supply. Beyond initial profit, there remained the satisfaction of observing the effect drugs had upon American society. Unchecked capitalism devoured itself in an orgy of criminal violence, vindicating the Marxist dialectic in bloody headlines.

The rest was a matter of convenience and strategy. If New Amsterdam made a convenient staging point for drug shipments abroad under the current regime, how much more useful would it be with a puppet government in power?

The candidate of choice was Armand Castillo, a native of New Amsterdam recruited by DGI—the Cuban secret service—in his youth. At nineteen, he had gone to live abroad in Moscow and Havana, training with the KGB at Patrice Lumumba University for foreign students in the

USSR. Eight months in Syria, training with Soviet-sponsored Palestinian guerrillas, had taught him the fine points of terrorism. CIA records indicated that Castillo had served a brief apprenticeship with the Sandinista rebels in Nicaragua before he returned home with ample money in his pocket to establish a successful chain of restaurants.

According to the Stony Man computer net, Castillo's start-up money had come from Moscow and Havana in the days before the Russian empire crumbled into ruins, but the Reds had also taught their man to pay his way by any means available. To that end, he had put out feelers to the major cocaine syndicate in Medellín, offering his services as a middleman in the traffic between Colombia and the United States. His fees were reasonable and a deal was made. The DEA had charted his cooperation with the cartel for more than two years, but Dutch authorities were hesitant to act without some evidence of local distribution on New Amsterdam. Thus far, that evidence was nonexistent, and Castillo's role in moving several thousand pounds of coke per year hadn't affected local crime rates in the least.

Until the Netherlands decided it was time New Amsterdam became an independent state.

The possibilities were obvious. A friendly government could pamper the cartel, expel American investigators and manipulate the banking laws to benefit the highest bidders. Short of military action, there was nothing the United States could do to stop New Amsterdam from becoming a combination drug depot, money laundry and haven for international fugitives. Castro meanwhile, would be laughing up his sleeve, the sole survivor of crumbling Soviet influence outside the Far East, contriving to expand his influence at the very time when international communism was being pronounced dead.

Armand Castillo had filed for the office of prime minister within two days of the announcement that independence was coming, a special election scheduled to install national officers pending adoption of a new constitution.

And with Castillo in power, Washington had no doubt the document produced by any constitutional convention would be tailored along socialist lines, with loopholes aplenty for the new prime minister's special friends abroad.

Castillo didn't have the field to himself, however. Within twenty-four hours of announcing his candidacy, the DGI mole had been challenged by one Martin Grandier, a fiery newspaperman in the old-style liberal tradition. Well-known as an opponent of corruption and a champion of civil rights, Grandier was also publisher and editor-in-chief of the *Journal*, New Amsterdam's second-largest daily paper. He had done his homework on Castillo, with some help from DEA, and while the bulk of what he learned was classified, there was enough for a series of stinging editorials that left Castillo fuming with rage.

Never one to suffer insults quietly, Castillo had responded on two levels with public denunciations of his opponent and a covert series of attacks that ranged from threats and ugly rumors to assaults on Grandier's campaign volunteers. There had been no fatalities before that morning but things were heating up—three drive-by shootings in the past eight days, a firebombing of Grandier's campaign office in Cranetown, plus escalating incidents of vandalism and harassment throughout the island. Grandier campaign workers had begun to fight back, despite their candidate's expressed commitment to nonviolence, but they were clearly outclassed by the talent available to Armand Castillo. Between Colombian muscle and thugs trained by the DGI, Castillo had a small army at his disposal, ready and willing to fight.

And that was where Bolan came in.

The emergency call from Brognola had found the Executioner between missions, a brief respite from action with several targets slated for consideration down the line. An hour's briefing on the rumble in New Amsterdam was all it took to sell him on the need for intervention now, before the votes were cast and the removal of Armand Castillo shifted from a street fight to a covert move against the head of state.

It had been years since Langley dabbled in "executive action," the polite euphemism for assassinating foreign politicians, and the President wasn't anxious for Hal Brognola's Stony Man team to pick up where the CIA had left off in another era. At the same time he deemed it essential that New Amsterdam's first independent government should be precisely that, beholden neither to the DGI nor the Colombian cartel. Ideally it would be preferred to let the people speak and reject Castillo and his covert allies but the latest polls were all too close to call.

It could go either way and Washington was worried that Castillo or his backers, in their desperation, might attempt to shift the odds through bribery or violence, even taking out Grandier himself if it came to that. There would be no time for a replacement candidate to file in that case and Castillo would carry the day by default, assured of six years at the helm before he stood for reelection.

Bolan had agreed to see what he could do and he had borrowed Rafael Encizo, usually a member of Phoenix Force, for the duration. Encizo was a Cuban transplant to the States and a committed enemy of Castro, expert in the workings of the DGI and Havana's time-honored tradition of exporting revolution to neighboring countries. A veteran counterterrorist, he would be especially valuable if they met any kind of opposition from Castillo's Cuban sponsors.

In the meantime though, Bolan's first priority was to establish contact. He had planned to stage a meeting with Alicia Grandier and introduce himself, but the initial plan had been scuttled by forces beyond his control. Now they had four members of the opposition dead and the stakes had been pushed through the ceiling.

It was do-or-die from this point forward and he knew Armand Castillo would be pulling out the stops; first retaliation, finally to cinch a big win on election day.

Bolan needed an edge. What he had at the moment was Alicia Grandier.

"Who are you?" she asked him as they fled the shooting scene, Encizo at the wheel.

"A friend," Bolan answered. "I think I can help."

"With guns?" Her tone was frankly skeptical but she didn't dismiss him out of hand.

"With any means available," he told her bluntly.

"I appreciate your help back there," Alicia said, "but this isn't our way. A victory by violence is defeat of everything my father stands for."

"I was thinking of survival," Bolan replied. "Those gunmen of Castillo's weren't about to let you walk away and run a peaceable campaign. They're turning up the heat and they won't stop till somebody gets burned."

"You are American," she said. "Who sent you to New Amsterdam?"

"Let's say I volunteered."

"Because you know my father and admire his work?"

"I won't pretend to be an expert on the local politics," Bolan stated, "but I know the opposition well enough to understand that with Castillo in control, your country won't be independent and the people won't be free."

"You value freedom, Mr...."

"Mike Belasko," he replied. "And I would have to say it beats the hell out of the alternative."

"The people must decide," Alicia told him, echoing her father's words.

"Assuming they're provided with a choice. What becomes of your democracy if someone takes your father out before election day or forces him to quit the race?"

Alicia flinched at the mention of her father's possible demise, then stiffened at the implication that he might abandon the campaign before election day.

"He wouldn't quit."

"Not even to preserve his daughter's life?"

She hesitated over that. "You mean to say..."

"If those four goons were looking for a body count they would have shot you on the street and driven on. The fact they tried to grab you means that they were looking for a hostage. Not just any hostage—you, the one volunteer they knew your father wouldn't sacrifice for principle."

Alicia thought about that for a moment. "Even so—"

"I need to meet your father," Bolan interrupted her. "He might not want to speak with me. His call. If that's the way it goes, so be it, but I have to try."

She hesitated. "You're asking me to trust you with my father's life."

"That's right."

"Because you just saved mine?"

The warrior shrugged. "It's all I have to trade right now."

Another moment passed before she said, "I have to use a telephone."

Encizo pulled into the next service station. They waited in the car while Alicia made her phone call, Bolan gambling that she wouldn't simply cut and run. It took the best part of five minutes and her attitude was cautious when she came back to the car.

"All right," she said. "My father has agreed to see you but his guards will have to hold your guns."

"Suits me," the Executioner replied.

She gave directions to Encizo, and the Cuban followed them precisely, making decent time in spite of morning traffic. Twenty minutes brought them to a small house in a northern suburb of the capital where several hard-eyed men were lined up waiting at the curb. In spite of Martin Grandier's avowed disdain for violence, Bolan saw that three of them were wearing pistols underneath their jackets.

"Wait here," he instructed Encizo, then trailed Alicia from the car. Two bodyguards fell into step on either side of him, a third behind, escorting him to the house. They walked around one side and frisked him only when a hedge prevented them from being glimpsed by passersby. He made no effort to resist as one of Grandier's protectors stuck the 93-R in his belt.

Inside, the house was tidy to a fault, as if reflecting Martin Grandier's well-known aversion to corruption and disorder even in the way his floors were swept and furniture arranged. Alicia led the way along a short hall to the study, knocked and entered. Bolan's three-man escort didn't follow them across the threshold, but he knew they would be waiting at the door, prepared to intervene at once if there was any hint of risk to their employer.

Martin Grandier was of average height and slender, with wire-rimmed glasses sliding down his nose. He pushed them back in place approximately once per minute in the time he spent with Bolan, simple movements taking on the aspect of a small, perhaps unconscious ritual.

"I understand you saved my daughter's life," Grandier said once they had shaken hands.

"It didn't start that way. Your opposition must be getting desperate."

"They fear defeat, this much we know. In any case, you have my gratitude."

"I need your help," Bolan said.

"To initiate a war against Castillo?"

"He's already started shooting, if you hadn't noticed. It won't help you to pretend the bullets don't exist."

"We have police to deal with any criminal offenses," Grandier replied.

"You see how well they've done so far."

The candidate stood firm. "I am in debt to you but I cannot allow you to subvert the course of our campaign. We will not sink to terrorism in the name of liberty."

"So, what's the party line on self-defense?"

Grandier frowned. "Violence spawns more violence, Mr. Belasko. Surely you have seen that in your own experience."

"Some adversaries don't speak any other language."

"They must be educated or restrained by rule of law," Grandier insisted.

"Your rule of law's not working very well right now and education won't be high up on Castillo's list of things to do. From what I saw today, he's out for blood."

"I cannot rule by violence," Grandier replied. "It would be futile for me to attempt a seizure of authority here in New Amsterdam."

"I was suggesting something more in line with leveling the odds," Bolan said. "As it is, you've got yourself outnumbered and outgunned."

"Perhaps."

"You know about Castillo's link to the Colombians." When Bolan spoke, it didn't come out sounding like a question.

"Yes."

"And what about Havana?"

"There are rumors, certainly. Perhaps, if I had more faith in the source..."

"I grant you, Langley has been known to paint things red from time to time without due cause," the Executioner allowed. "This time I'd say they've got it straight."

"And if the Cubans are involved, what then?" Grandier asked. "It's impossible to cancel the election now."

"Nobody mentioned cancellation," Bolan said. "I'm talking strategy for winning."

"With a gun?"

"With you and yours alive." He cast a sidelong glance toward where Alicia Grandier had settled in a straight-backed chair and found her watching him. "If it comes down to do-or-die, you'll have to make a choice. It helps if there's some preparation in advance."

"I understand you wouldn't tell my daughter who has sent you here. I must repeat the question."

"You have friends you aren't aware of yet," Bolan said.

"Friends in Washington?"

"And elsewhere, I suspect."

"Who send me gunmen on the eve of our first national election in New Amsterdam. I cannot help but wonder what the price for such assistance may turn out to be."

"As far as I'm concerned, it's on the house."

"And you speak with full authority?" Grandier asked.

"I know the people who can answer that if you're concerned."

The candidate was frowning as he shook his head. "There is no need," he said. "The price I see before me is too high."

"For the election or your daughter's life?"

"As I've already said, you have my gratitude. There can be nothing more between us."

Bolan understood that he was talking to a man of stubborn principles—the next thing to a stout brick wall. It had been worth a shot but he was wasting time. But if he tried another tack ...

"At least consider this," Bolan said. "In the car, outside, I have a friend. He's Cuban, well acquainted with the DGI, their operations, anything you'd ever want to know about Fidel from *A* to *Z*. I'd like to leave him here with you—on loan, let's say—to help you spot the opposition if and when they come around."

"You'll pardon me if I suspect your motives," Grandier replied.

"Of course. Take your time and think about it. Hold his weapon if you like. Another pair of eyes could only help you out."

"That would depend on what your friend is looking for and who receives the benefit of any observations he should make."

"That's fair enough," Bolan said. "For the record, I don't need an eye inside your team. The papers tell me all I need to know about your movements. I could set my watch by your appearances...and so could anybody else."

"Campaigning for elected office still requires some contact with the people," Grandier reminded him. "If it were otherwise, there would be little hope for freedom in the land."

"At least consider my proposal, in the interest of security."

"On the condition that your friend is under my authority exclusively. He must refrain from any violence. If he cannot control himself, I will deliver him to the police."

"I'll make it clear," the Executioner agreed.

"And you? What can I say to ward off any further violence?"

"You might try prayer," Bolan suggested, "but I wouldn't hold my breath."

2

The high-rise office building was part of Hollandia's new image, putting a modern face on paradise. While modest by American standards, barely sixteen stories tall, it was a landmark in the capital, all burnished steel and glass.

A long block to the east, Mack Bolan stretched out on the rooftop of another high-rise, staring at the office complex through a telescopic sight. His full attention focused on the seventh floor, third window from the southeast corner.

He was watching out for a familiar face.

The Walther WA-2000 is a state-of-the-art sniper's weapon crafted with portability and optimum efficiency in mind. Constructed in the bullpup design, with its 6-round magazine and gas-operated bolt mechanism mounted behind the trigger group, it measures slightly less than three feet overall from padded butt to muzzle. The twenty-five-inch barrel is clamped at front and rear to prevent lift on firing, fluted along its full length to provide extra cooling surface and minimize vibrations that detract from accuracy. Bolan's weapon was chambered for the classic Winchester .300 Magnum cartridge and fitted with a 10-power Schmidt & Bender scope.

When it was broken down, the Walther fit inside a metal toolbox which rested at his left side on the roof. The coveralls he wore were faded denim, nondescript, a workman's uniform. No one had given him a second glance when Bolan parked the rented van downstairs and rode the service elevator up eleven floors. Two flights of dingy stairs had brought him to the rooftop where a tenant might assume that he was working on the bulky air conditioners or exhaust fans.

A hundred yards distant, the target zone was crystal clear. The architects hadn't employed reflective glass but rather settled for the barest smoky tint. The Schmidt & Bender scope made Bolan feel as if he were inside the room.

And at the moment he was all alone.

He scanned the desks and walls, the filing cabinets, wet bar, padded chairs—the trappings of a young executive, already affluent but still in transit to the pinnacle of ultimate success. A casual observer couldn't guess his business from a glance around the room but Bolan knew his target inside out.

The man who occupied that office was a ranking member of the Medellín cartel.

Specifically his name was Pablo Obregon, age twenty-eight. His older brother called the shots in Medellín and lately in New Amsterdam where dealings with Armand Castillo were concerned. Both brothers faced indictments in the States but the Colombian authorities had trouble finding them these days. New Amsterdam had served them well and they harbored great plans for the future, once Castillo was installed to lead the independent government.

Meanwhile, the Executioner had other plans.

He saw the office door swing open, four men filing through before it closed again. The tallest of the four was Pablo Obregon, his sharp face oscillating as if he was trying to sniff out a mouse in the room. He took a seat behind the massive desk and leaned back in his chair, waiting for the others to arrange themselves in front of him; a captive audience.

Bolan was no lip-reader but he didn't have to guess what Pablo and his cronies were discussing. Any business transacted in that office was drug-related, one way or another, and it made no difference if the dirty money filtered into politics, religion or the most exalted charity.

Blood money never lost its taint and dealers never spent a dime without expecting half a dollar's profit in return.

So he had come to interrupt a business meeting, make his presence felt among the enemy without allowing them to glimpse his face or grasp his motives.

The piece was sighted for one hundred fifty yards. He chose a target, calculating the projectile's rise at eight-tenths of an inch over one hundred yards, and checked his sights accordingly. The 180-grain bullets would be traveling at roughly 2,745 feet per second when they reached their targets, imparting more than 3,000 foot-pounds of destructive energy on impact.

The Walther was rock solid on its bipod, the stock smooth and cool against Bolan's right cheek. He took a deep breath, released half of it and swallowed to lock in the rest. His pulse was audible, a steady drumbeat, as his index finger curled around the trigger, taking up the slack.

Downrange, his target smiled.

THE WEEK HAD STARTED WELL for Pablo Obregon. They had another shipment in from Medellín; two thousand kilos waiting to be cut and shipped from Cranetown to the States and that meant cash in hand. A major portion of the profits would be funneled into the Castillo war chest, an investment in the future, but Pablo understood that you had to spend money to make money.

It was part of the natural law.

The election was two weeks away and the campaign had been heating up all over New Amsterdam. Pablo knew it troubled his brother, Francisco, that the polls were too close to call, but Pablo wasn't worried. Money talked and bullshit walked, in politics as in all other fields of human enterprise. On rare occasions when the money wasn't talking loud enough, you either raised the ante or applied strategic muscle to improve the opposition's hearing.

Money. Muscle. It was all the same, means to an end, where the high rollers came out on top and the peasants went hungry.

Like always.

The three men ranged in front of Pablo Obregon were middle management in the cartel he operated with his brother. Bernardo Reynosa was a fixer, skilled at making money whisper in the proper ears. He wore a politician's unctuous smile and combed his hair straight back from a squarish face. Lupe Moreno was a mover, one of half a dozen ranking experts the cartel employed to keep its product flowing day by day, around the clock, without a problem. Salvador Ybarra was a cold, man-eating shark, renowned in Medellín as one of the prominent assassins of the past two decades. Short and lean, he held a black belt in karate and was ambidextrous with small arms.

Reynosa was explaining why they didn't have to sweat the polls at the moment, no matter what the papers and the television said. Behind the scenes, where deals and victories were made, the cartel's money was at work subverting judges, law enforcement, legislators. Even if Castillo lost the race somehow, his opposition would be one man sitting in the office trying to perform while those about him took their orders from the Obregon brothers.

It brought a fleeting smile to Pablo's face, imagining that outcome, how the Cubans would be pissed at watching one more dream of revolution blown away. He didn't nurse the image long, however, since he knew Francisco had a bargain with Havana. If the deal was suddenly aborted there would be hell to pay.

"We need the win," he told Reynosa. "Don't start planning on a loss when we've got two weeks left before the vote, okay?"

Reynosa almost lost his smile at that but saved it in the crunch. "Of course not, Pablo. All I'm saying is—"

They would have to guess, forever after, what he was about to say. Before his lips could form the words, there was a popping, cracking sound.

His ears had barely registered the noise when Pablo saw the lower portion of Reynosa's face explode. One moment Bernardo was speaking to him in a level tone of voice and then his jaw disintegrated with a red, wet, ripping sound, erupting in a spray of teeth, bone and mutilated flesh.

The jolting impact hurled Reynosa to his left and dropped his mutilated head into Salvador Ybarra's lap. It was a spectacle of sorts, the human shark recoiling, rising from his chair, blood soaking through his slacks from belt to knees. Instinctively, Ybarra thrust a hand inside his jacket, reaching for the pistol that he always wore beneath one arm.

He never made it.

Pablo Obregon was still attempting to assimilate Bernardo Reynosa's death when something punched Ybarra over on his back. There was a solid sound of impact, crimson spouting from the gunner's chest.

The dealer knew exactly what was happening in that split second. They were under fire, long distance, maybe with a silencer, some kind of trick-shot artist showing off at Obregon's expense.

He kicked his chair back and dived for the carpet, slow enough to glimpse Lupe Moreno's final moments of life. He was rising from his chair, cursing in amazement, when the whole top of his skull took flight without him, trailing hair and flecks of gray matter. The mover stood rock steady for a heartbeat, dead before he knew it, then slowly toppled over on his face.

The desk was solid teak and weighed a ton. When Obregon rolled underneath it, he felt safe from anything... until the hammering began.

The first round struck his chair and sent it spinning backward, bouncing it off the nearest wall. He saw it topple forward, slamming down twelve to fifteen inches from his face.

Round two punched through a corner of the desk and popped the upper right-hand drawer completely off its runners, spewing pencils and stationery.

Round three slapped hard against the desk, low down, and for an instant Pablo thought that it was coming through to find him in his little cave. In fact, the desk held firm and he was saved.

A lull, the seconds bleeding into minutes, and he lay there trembling, pinned beneath his desk afraid to move. At last he realized that it was over, wriggling out just far enough to reach the intercom. A woman's voice responded from the waiting room outside his soundproof office.

"Yes, sir, Mr. Obregon?"

"We're getting killed in here, goddammit!" Pablo shouted from his hidey-hole. "I want some guns up here right now!"

ONE MAJOR STAGING POINT for foreign muscle in New Amsterdam was a walled estate outside Hollandia, due south along the coast. The DEA had scoped it out with aerial surveillance photos when the Obregons arrived and set up shop. The house was large enough for twenty-five or thirty soldiers if they packed in like sardines but recent estimates put roughly half the larger number currently in residence. Of those, perhaps one-third were constantly on duty in Hollandia.

That made perhaps ten soldiers on the grounds, then, twelve at the outside—assuming DEA's intelligence was accurate.

Bolan parked the gray sedan a quarter mile beyond the wrought-iron gates, along a narrow side road that was hidden from the coastal highway by a stand of trees. Another moment saw him changed from street clothes into camouflage fatigues and military webbing with a nylon camo ski mask covering his face. His weapons were a mixed bag from the Ka-bar fighting knife to the Beretta 93-R worn beneath his arm, the .44 Magnum Desert Eagle autoloader on his hip and the folding-stock Uzi submachine gun slung across his shoulder. Extra magazines for all three weapons filled the pouches at his waist and the bandolier across his chest. Four compact fragmentation grenades completed the ensemble, leaving Bolan literally dressed to kill.

He walked back through the spotty woods, taking advantage of the natural camouflage wherever possible, moving at a steady pace over open ground when there was no alternative. It took him twenty minutes to retrace his path and reach his target zone.

The south wall of the hardsite was approximately eight feet high with no broken glass or razor wire on top to slow him down. It was an easy climb and Bolan used a silent whistle to assure himself there were no guard dogs on patrol before he made the final drop inside.

He skirted the open lawn, keeping to the fringe of trees and bushes near the wall until he had a clear view of the patio and swimming pool behind the two-story house. Three men were lounging there in bathing suits, two others splashing in the pool. Four cars were parked out front and granting that the hitters wouldn't have a vehicle apiece, what did that mean in terms of guns on-site?

Bolan knew there was only one way to find out.

He came in for them at an angle, finger on the Uzi's trigger, shooting frequent glances toward the house as he approached. The windows stared back at him, blank and lifeless. No one sounded an alarm.

The gunners were relaxed but not entirely unprepared. As the warrior neared the pool, he saw that two of them had shoulder holsters draped across the backrests of their deck chairs, close at hand. The swimmers were unarmed, of course, but it was one of them who spotted him while climbing from the pool.

The shooter did a startled double take, at first refusing to believe his eyes. He shouted a warning in Spanish, his index finger pointing toward the new arrival, when a 3-round burst of parabellum manglers struck him in the chest and pitched him back into the pool.

The Uzi had no silencer and its staccato voice immediately galvanized the four surviving hardmen. Those at poolside scrambled to their feet, two reaching for their holstered weapons while the third man sprinted for the house. The sole surviving swimmer started for the nearest ladder that would put him high and dry.

He had a choice to make and Bolan worked on instinct: take the armed men first. His Uzi stuttered, tracking left to right with two short bursts dispatched from fifteen yards. The gunner on his left jerked through an awkward little dance and dropped his shoulder holster with the side arm still secured in leather, falling to his knees before he toppled over, lifeless, on his face.

The second shooter had his pistol out but there was no time left for him to use it as a burst of parabellum shockers stitched him from his navel to his clavicle. The impact punched him over backward and he sprawled on the deck, mere inches from the pool. His pistol spun away from lifeless fingers, overshot the edge and plunked into the water.

The distracted swimmer saw it, made a desperate change of course to intercept, and Bolan left him to it for the moment, tracking on the runner who had almost reached his goal.

Another burst from the warrior's submachine gun helped him get there, lifting him completely off his feet and slamming him face first into the broad glass sliding doors. They shattered as momentum carried him across the threshold, dead before he landed on the carpeting inside what seemed to be a recreation room.

Four down and one remaining.

Bolan turned back toward the swimming pool in time to see the swimmer dive. He waited, conscious of potential danger from the house, determined not to leave an armed and dangerous enemy behind him.

A cloud of bubbles broke the surface with the gunner following. He came up firing blind, eyes open, streaming chlorinated water, pumping three rounds toward the sky before he found his target several yards away and to his left.

Too late.

The Uzi spit another short precision burst and Bolan watched another crimson stain begin to spread across the surface of the water. They were dead shots, quick and clean. No need for him to wait and check for signs of life.

He palmed a frag grenade and turned back toward the house. It might be overkill but he didn't believe in taking needless chances. Bolan dropped the pin at thirty feet, wound up the pitch and sailed it through the open doorway from the patio, a long shot to the far side of the rec room past the dead man sprawling in the entryway.

Sidestepping, flattening himself against the deck, he waited for the blast. Hot shrapnel whispered across the patio, most of it ripping through the inside walls and ceiling. Smoke and plaster dust provided him some cover as he slipped inside the house.

Someone was cursing in the middle distance, possibly one room away, and speaking in heated Spanish. That meant two of them, at least, if they were talking. Bolan moved in the direction of the voices, leading with his Uzi, ready to respond with sudden death the moment that an adversary showed himself.

They met him coming through a hallway from the dining room and kitchen, one man carrying an MP-5 K submachine gun while the other had a pistol in each hand. Bolan had a heartbeat, give or take, in which to save himself before they opened fire and there was no time left for meditating over which one should die first.

He let his Uzi do the talking, pouring out a spiral burst that cleared the magazine and sent the runners reeling in a storm of parabellum rounds, blood spattering the walls around them as they fell. Both men were quick enough to use their weapons but the rounds went high and wide, except for one that traced a line of fire across the Executioner's left thigh.

Reloading on the move, he stepped across the tangled, prostrate bodies, scouting the hallway for other signs of life. There were no voices but he heard a furtive, scuffling noise somewhere ahead of him, drawing him onward in search of the source.

The sounds were much closer now, near a closet on his left, like some gigantic rodent shifting in its nest. A man-sized rat perhaps.

He stepped to one side of the closet, stretching out his left arm to deliver a resounding slap against the door. Immediately four quick pistol shots drilled through the panel, slicing empty air before they struck the wall directly opposite.

A short step forward, and the Uzi did the rest, stitching a tall letter *Z* on the door from chest height to floor level. Bolan heard the impact of a body slumping to the floor and he unleashed another short burst through the panel prior to opening the door.

The young man sprawled at his feet was all of twenty but the automatic pistol in his hand made all the difference in the world. It might not be an equalizer in the truest sense but it was close enough to make him dangerous—and all it took to get him killed.

The house was silent now and Bolan didn't take the time required to search the upper floor. If he had overlooked survivors, they would serve him as messengers to warn the Obregons of lethal opposition from a source unknown.

It was the best that he could hope for at the moment, striking at Armand Castillo's drug connection while avoiding contact with the candidate himself. The warrior couldn't initiate any action that would place Castillo in a sympathetic light and cast a shadow over Martin Grandier as a potential terrorist.

It was a fine line, granted, but the Executioner had played that kind of game before. He hadn't been defeated yet, but each time out the rules were different. New adversaries meant new strategies, revised to fit the game.

He used two more of the grenades in parting. One went in the ground-floor bathroom which ripped through the water main and set off a flood that would destroy the downstairs carpeting if nothing else. The other, Bolan pitched into the oven from a distance after turning on the gas, retreating in a sprint before the kitchen went up in a churning ball of flame.

The Obregons would need another hardsite for their soldiers. It would be a minor inconvenience, when he thought about it, but the raid might draw attention from authorities. If not, it was enough to let the opposition know they didn't have the game all to themselves.

3

For Rafael Encizo, stepping out unarmed felt rather like appearing naked on the public street. In fact, experience had taught him that it would be safer minus trousers than without a weapon.

One would get you laughed at, possibly arrested, while the other could get you killed.

Still, there was little choice once Bolan struck his deal with Martin Grandier. The candidate agreed to let Encizo—or "Raul Camacho"—tag along as watchdog, but the ground rules were established going in—no guns or other weapons, no aggressive violence, no reports to Mike Belasko that hadn't been cleared through Grandier.

The last provision would be difficult, if not impossible for Grandier and company to monitor, but they had frisked Encizo on arrival and relieved him of his side arm, plus a five-foot boot knife. They had overlooked a small push-dagger disguised as a belt buckle but Encizo still felt vulnerable.

It was no good taking a knife to a gunfight, especially when your opponents had already shown a willingness to kill.

Their mission for the early afternoon was hanging posters and distributing campaign leaflets at a downtown shopping mall. It sounded boring but the one fringe benefit turned out to be Alicia Grandier. Perhaps she was assigned to keep a sharp eye on Encizo, or she might have planned to join the group in any case, but the little Cuban was pleased to learn that she would be close by.

It helped him watch one member of the family at least, and not long after she had been selected for a kidnapping attempt. If he couldn't be everywhere at once, at least he had Alicia under scrutiny.

At the same time there was something else. He felt strongly attracted to Alicia Grandier, however unprofessional that was, and watching her would be a pleasant duty, even in the most adverse conditions.

Encizo was a professional above all else and he wouldn't allow his feelings to subvert performance of the task at hand. But if he had a chance to mix business with pleasure before all hell broke loose, then why not take advantage of the opportunity?

The four of them went downtown in a van with Martin Grandier's likeness painted larger than life on each side. Alicia drove, Encizo in the shotgun seat, with two male volunteers behind them. He could feel the others watching him, as if they half expected him to bail out in the midst of traffic, run amok with total strangers on the street.

"Have you done this kind of thing before?" Alicia asked.

Encizo frowned. "What kind of thing?"

"Campaigning."

"Years ago," he said. "Around Miami when the Fidelistas made believe that they had changed in hope that Washington would recognize the Castro government."

"You were successful?"

"At the time," he replied. "Times change."

"But for the better, I believe."

"That would depend upon the changes. I don't see anybody better off in Bosnia since Yugoslavia broke up."

"That was regressive change," she argued. "Whenever violence is included, progress suffers."

"You've been getting beat up pretty bad the past few weeks from what I understand."

"The people see and understand who is responsible for bloodshed in the streets. They will remember on election day."

"But which way will they vote?" Encizo asked.

"For peace, of course." She seemed amused at his naiveté. "A vote for violence would defeat self-interest."

"Maybe so." His tone was frankly skeptical.

"You disagree?"

"I've seen elections carried by the bribe, the bomb, the bullet," he replied. "It doesn't always work out that the good guys win."

"Perhaps in other places," Alicia said stiffly. "We have laws here in New Amsterdam."

"I guess those men who tried to snatch you off the street this morning never read the law."

"I'm not afraid," she told him, bright eyes flaming. "After we have won our victory, the violent men will have no place among us."

Wishful thinking, Encizo decided, but he kept it to himself. Instead, he said, "I hope you're right."

"You'll see."

They traveled another block then she turned left into a smallish parking lot. The mall wasn't large by U.S. standards, thirty-five or forty stores with only two or three of any size, but it was obviously doing major business even in the middle of the day. There were more bicycles than cars in evidence as well as pedestrians arriving and departing in a steady stream. Encizo estimated that there had to be roughly three hundred shoppers in the mall.

Alicia found a parking space and Encizo went EVA. He walked behind the van and waited for his two male escorts to emerge to unload rolled-up posters and leaflets by the box. The little Cuban took his share, a roll of posters underneath one arm, a heavy box beneath the other, and fell into step beside Alicia, moving as she headed toward the mall.

"I hope you aren't about to let me down," she told him seriously.

Encizo responded with a smile. "I promise that's the last thing on my mind."

ALICIA GRANDIER COULDN'T explain her feelings for the man who called himself Raul Camacho. Not that she supposed it was his name—if he was prone to carry guns and shoot at total strangers on the street, then lying would be second nature, part of daily life.

Still, there was something. . . .

He was handsome in a rugged fashion, there was no denying that. Of course, she didn't find him physically attractive. That would be bizarre, like something from a romance novel—girl meets savage, hoping to redeem him, and gets swept away by primitive emotion.

Stuff and nonsense.

More than anything, he frightened her, almost as much as she was frightened by his friend, the gunman known as Mike Belasko. They were two of a kind and Alicia shuddered to think of the crimes they had witnessed, the things they had done.

To what end?

Belasko's intervention on her behalf that morning seemed to be an act of generosity but there were clearly hidden motives. He had sought to infiltrate her father's party and subvert his mission with a violent twist: retaliation in the name of self-defense, revenge exalted over reason and the rule of law.

She had been proud to see her father standing fast against Belasko's argument despite the recent peril to herself. They all made sacrifices for the cause in one way or another and Alicia knew the risks before she had agreed to help with the campaign. She felt a certain gratitude to Mike Belasko, certainly, but that was only natural. It didn't mean that she endorsed his violent course of action or his plan for carrying the so-called war against their enemies.

The people of New Amsterdam would choose their leader at the polls as it was meant to be. They wouldn't be deceived by lies, suborned by bribes or frightened off by men with guns.

Inside the mall she spent a moment with the others, pairing off to make the best use of their time. Camacho would accompany her while Thomas and his cousin Vin-

cent worked the far end of the complex, touching base with
as many shoppers as possible over the next ninety minutes.

"This way."

She led Camacho to a small men's-clothing shop and
went inside. The owner was an old friend of her father's
and he had agreed to display a poster in his windows if it
didn't block the view of suits on sale. Camacho stood and
watched while she exchanged brief pleasantries with the
proprietor then helped her tape a poster in the lower right-
hand corner of the window just beside the door where any
entering customers would have to see it.

The other shop proprietors they spoke to in the mall
each had an impeccable excuse for refusing to display a
poster. When you boiled them down to basics, it was always business—whatever their opinion of Martin Grandier, they wouldn't risk losing customers by jumping into
partisan politics—but here and there Alicia caught a hint
of something else.

Intimidation.

It was visible in furtive glances, trembling fingertips, the
barest stutter when a certain individual began to speak.
Among the frightened, she began to notice that their answers sounded pat, rehearsed. It took some time for her to
understand exactly what was happening, but once the
mental link was made, she had no problem judging for
herself who was responsible.

A sudden flash of anger warmed her cheeks. Alicia was
uncomfortable with the feeling, raised as she had been to
cope nonviolently with situations where injustice was the
rule. But she couldn't suppress the urge to lash out at her
father's enemies in some way other than a speech or pam-
phlet—something physical which they would all remember for a good long time.

She glanced at Raul Camacho wondering how many
arms and noses he had broken in his time, how many lives
he had extinguished. Looking at him, feeling mixed emotions of attraction for the man and grim repulsion for his
stock-in-trade, she understood that it would be a rela-

tively simple thing to yield and give free rein to her emotions—satisfy her momentary anger with destructive action when the proper course was to reorganize, rethink their campaign strategy and find a way around the momentary stalemate.

First though, there were leaflets to be handed out, her father's message to be shared with men and women she had never met before and likely never would again. Most took the pamphlets without comment, though Alicia knew that half of them at least would drop her father's message in the nearest trash can once they felt it could be done without an overt show of rudeness. Of the ones who read her father's words, how many would be moved to vote for him in two weeks' time?

Alicia tried not to consider the disturbing prospect of defeat, what it would mean not only to her father but New Amsterdam. She concentrated on the act of handing leaflets out to passersby, speaking to those who would talk, smiling at those in a hurry. They had been at work for twenty minutes, more or less, when suddenly there was no one around her. Glancing at her companion, she saw him stiffen, staring over her shoulder at something or someone behind her.

Alicia turned and found herself confronted with the enemy, four burly men, of whom she recognized Ramon Gutierrez, the leader.

RAMON GUTIERREZ WAS listed as "executive campaign coordinator" on the payroll of Armand Castillo's Independence Party. If the truth were known, Gutierrez had no more to do with planning the campaign from day to day than a gorilla has to do with the administration of a zoo in which he lives. He was adept at hurting people and destroying property, twin skills acquired during a misspent youth and channeled by his handlers in the Cuban DGI.

Gutierrez was an agent, though his intellect wouldn't have qualified him as a spy per se. Collection and transmission of intelligence wasn't his strong suit. Rather, he was much more likely to be sent in search of those who failed at their more subtle duties—traitors, double agents, even simple cowards who allowed cold feet to put them off their game. He had been schooled in mayhem with a smattering of languages and codes to make his covert education more well-rounded, but his specialty was still intimidation—or elimination—of selected targets.

His assignment to Armand Castillo was a deviation for Gutierrez. So far, he hadn't been called upon to murder anybody in New Amsterdam, but it was coming. He could feel it. There were plans in progress that Gutierrez didn't even know about, dark business with the men from Medellín, but that didn't concern him. He took orders from Havana and his orders were to help Armand Castillo seize the ruling power in New Amsterdam. A second aspect of his mission, never mentioned to the candidate, required Gutierrez to observe Castillo and to report any evidence that he intended to betray Havana's interest for a personal reward. The Fidelistas didn't care if he got rich from graft and drug sales; they expected nothing less. But if Castillo tried to cheat his masters, then Ramon Gutierrez was to terminate the traitor.

Meanwhile, he had mundane assignments to perform, such as harassment of the volunteers supporting Martin Grandier's campaign and disruption of his media machine wherever possible. That afternoon he had received a tip from an informant in the other camp that Grandier's daughter was leading a team to the New Market Mall attempting to corral more votes.

It was an opportunity Gutierrez couldn't miss and he decided to attend and supervise the confrontation personally. If nothing else, it would get him out of the office, away from the telephone's incessant ringing and people asking him to run all kinds of stupid errands. He could use a little action.

He chose three sluggers from the pool of talent recruited upon his arrival in Hollandia. They were ignorant types, fond of money and rum, willing to do most anything on a promise of one or the other. They were useful men when it came down to breaking legs or heads, defacing property or tossing gasoline bombs through the windows of a home or office. Never mind who suffered in the process, just as long as they were paid.

Ramon's kind of people, in short.

And best of all, they were disposable.

When he ran across Alicia Grandier, he put on his best sarcastic smile.

"Good afternoon, Miss Grandier," he said. "We meet again."

"Too soon for my taste," she replied.

Gutierrez chuckled, shaking his head. "Such hostility in one so young. You should be careful of your temper."

"Almost being kidnapped makes me angry. I suppose you find that strange?"

Gutierrez was completely in the dark as to her meaning. Perhaps the Colombians, with their persistent knack for meddling in affairs that didn't rightfully concern them, had accosted her. If Castillo needed two enforcement squads, he should have told Havana at the start and more men would have been provided. As it was, Gutierrez sometimes felt that he was operating in an echo chamber where the same instructions had been given twice or even three times, effort duplicated—wasted—by redundant teams.

In this case, though, he had Alicia and her flunky to himself.

"I must object to the insinuation," Gutierrez replied. "In fact, I must object most strenuously. You have wounded my companions to the core. It is beyond me to restrain them when they feel this way."

So saying, he stepped back and motioned for the sluggers to proceed. It should be simple, one man and a woman against three. Gutierrez could always help out his men if they had any difficulty with the job.

Meanwhile, he would enjoy the show.

ENCIZO WAS READY when the three goons made their move. He put the leader out of mind for the moment, concentrating on the shock troops, choosing his targets in order of size and approach.

The three hardmen ranged in height from roughly five foot eight to six foot one or two, with Encizo on eye level with the shortest of the three. Each man outweighed him by an average of thirty pounds, their biceps straining at the seams of short-sleeved shirts, legs slightly bowed as if from carrying the weight of barrel torsos. He had seen their kind before, in street fights and in prison yards. They would be tough opponents, granted, but their eyes betrayed a common emptiness that told him they were far from being intellectuals.

Alicia was prepared to stand her ground but Encizo removed her from the center of the action with a firm hand on her shoulder and a sharp tug backward. He stepped forward to meet his adversaries, choosing the tallest of the three, immediately on his right, because he sought to make a point—and, incidentally, because a straight move on the middleman would put him in the midst of a gorilla sandwich.

Feinting to the left, he pivoted and brought his foot down on the tall man's instep with sufficient force to crack the bone. His adversary cursed and staggered backward, losing balance, while Encizo took advantage of the moment, boring in. He snapped an elbow toward the slugger's face, connected with his nose and felt the cartilage implode. It wasn't a killing stroke, but it released twin jets of blood and dazzled Encizo's opponent with the rush of sudden pain.

Retreating from the first move, with Number One still on his feet, Encizo faced the others, taking up a limber combat stance. The goons regarded him with obvious contempt and rushed at him together, cursing on their injured friend's behalf.

Encizo ducked a roundhouse swing and drove four stiffened fingers underneath the middle-sized hardman's ribs, ignoring pain as rigid muscle met his thrust. No matter how it hurt his hand, the guy on the receiving end was feeling worse. He doubled over, clutching at his side and gasping, nearly going down on one knee as he grappled with the pain.

The little Cuban took advantage of the lapse and came in with a forearm to the slugger's jawline, putting all his weight behind it, striking with a vengeance. He could feel the jaw crack, twisting out of line, teeth grating, chipping. Consciousness deserted his opponent in a flare of pain, with darkness running close behind, and Encizo stepped back to let him fall.

That left one hardman in good condition while the first one tried to get his bearings and come back for more. Encizo concentrated on the fit opponent first, circling, watching the bad boy's hands for weapons or any sudden move. At the same time he was conscious of the puppet master on the sidelines, watching with distaste and obviously itching for a chance to join the fight before security arrived.

How long before the leader waded in?

Encizo put it out of his mind and concentrated on the task at hand.

The slugger rushed him and Encizo did the opposite of what a seasoned fighter would expect. Instead of backing off, he moved to meet the charge and snapped a short kick toward his adversary's groin. The hardman deflected it with a thick wrist, but he was focused on his precious genitals just long enough for Encizo to finish off the move—a pivot on his left foot, with the right heel orbiting his body, lashing into his opponent's temple with the power of a baseball bat connecting with a fastball at the plate. Explosive impact dropped the slugger on his side and left him twitching there as Encizo went back to finish Number One.

It was a simple thing, although the big man saw him coming, swollen eyes betraying pain and something very much like fear. The hitter raised both hands to guard his face and Encizo went in beneath them, taking out his left knee with a raking kick that left the big man groveling in pain. A rabbit punch behind the ear was all it took to put him down.

And that left the observer on the sidelines, glaring red faced at the ruin of his team.

"Your move," Encizo told him, waiting.

Swallowing his pride together with a heavy dose of bile, Gutierrez shook his head and answered, "Not today, I think."

And in that moment, listening, Encizo pegged him as a Cuban.

DGI? What else, if he was working for Armand Castillo?

"Maybe next time," Encizo suggested, "if you bring your nerve along."

"Next time indeed."

Encizo took Alicia by the arm and led her from the battlefield before security arrived to tie them up with questions. Let the opposition get stuck with the interrogation, if they couldn't pull their act together.

The game was under way in earnest now, and with Mack Bolan, he had drawn first blood. It would become more difficult from that point on, but difficulty only meant more effort was required.

Encizo smiled, anticipating action down the line.

4

Armand Castillo knew he was in trouble but he couldn't say as yet how bad the situation was. The failed attempt to grab Alicia Grandier had cost his side four lives. Two other shooting incidents had claimed eleven more. To put the frosting on the cake, Ramon Gutierrez and three of his men had been humiliated by a Grandier campaign volunteer at the New Market Mall. They had avoided being jailed, but that was the only positive note in an otherwise hideous day.

And now, on top of everything, he had been summoned by Francisco Obregon.

It was predictable, of course. The fifteen dead men all belonged to Obregon. They were assassins, soldiers in his drug cartel, transported to New Amsterdam as part of Obregon's attempt to grab the island for himself.

Castillo cherished no illusions in regard to who was running his campaign. His first allegiance theoretically was to Havana, but the Cubans had encouraged him to deal with Obregon and company for weapons, cash, what an American would doubtless call "the whole nine yards." He understood that certain Fidelistas were also making tidy profits from the traffic in cocaine the Obregons were smuggling through New Amsterdam to the United States, fattening their wallets at the same time as they struck a pose for "people's revolution" in the Western Hemisphere.

It was a lot of nonsense, thought Castillo. You could call it anything you wanted to, but money was the bottom line. When Castro grabbed power in 1959, he had been quick to purge the gangsters from Havana, closing their casinos, executing pimps and jailing prostitutes. There had been no accommodation for the underworld, despite persistent rumors of a standing multimillion-dollar bribe.

Times change.

These days Castro had no support from Moscow or the shattered Warsaw Pact. He stood alone, hemmed in by governments who had rejected communism at the outset or else tried it for a little while before degenerating into chaos. More and more, Havana's rebel leader had the aspect of a dinosaur that had outlived its time. Unable or unwilling to simply lie down and die, the creature snarled and thrashed and beat the bushes for potential prey.

And found New Amsterdam.

Drug money was a huge shot in the arm, and after running merchandise directly out of Cuba for a time—an effort soon unraveled and revealed to public scrutiny by agents of the DEA—it was decided that an "independent" client state would better serve the needs of all concerned. Castro could shrug and issue his denials of complicity. The Obregons could hide out on New Amsterdam, secure against American indictments while a friendly face presided at the helm of government.

Castillo understood all this and none of it was news to him. He had resigned himself to being used as long as he could get rich in the process. So far, it was working, but the best was yet to come—as long as no one from the outside interfered and spoiled his plan.

It had to be outsiders, thought Castillo. Martin Grandier was dedicated to nonviolence—on the public record, anyway—and he had never shown the slightest tendency toward physical retaliation in the past, no matter what the threat to his security.

But could the attempted kidnap of his daughter finally have pushed Grandier over the edge? And if so, how was a peaceable man able to strike back so quickly, so efficiently, on so many fronts?

Outsiders, definitely. But who? From where? And why?

The U.S. government would clearly have an interest in subverting Castillo's campaign and installing Grandier as prime minister of New Amsterdam, but would Washington go to this extent, initiating bloodshed in the streets? Castillo, as a graduate of training in Havana and in Moscow, knew exactly what the old CIA had been willing to do in its war against Castro. He had also seen the KGB and DGI at work, up close and personal, but those days were gone.

At least in theory.

Castillo's driver slowed for the approach to Obregon's estate. They were two miles outside Hollandia, due west, an easy fifteen minutes from the national airport. Obregon also had his own airstrip on the estate for private visitors and those deliveries he didn't want disturbed by customs, but the dealer liked to hedge his bets.

The access road was paved with asphalt, Obregon's concession to his love of shiny cars. It ran for roughly three hundred yards with forest pressing close on either side. Castillo had no doubt that he was being watched on the approach. It was expected of a wealthy fugitive that he would take precautions for his own security.

They cleared the trees a moment later, Castillo's driver following the long, curved driveway that completely circled Obregon's palatial home away from home. The parking area was out in back. Nobody parked in front because Francisco thought it spoiled the new arrival's first impression of his house.

Castillo sat and waited while his driver killed the limo's engine, then circled the vehicle to open his door. Before he had a chance to brush the wrinkles from his slacks, Francisco's houseman was beside him, smiling.

"Good afternoon, sir. Please follow me. Mr. Obregon is waiting for you in the study."

MACK BOLAN WAS WAITING for Castillo, too, but not in the study. In fact, he was a hundred yards from the house, concealed amid some ferns and bushes on the east side of the clearing that included Obregon's manor house, outbuildings, helipad, tennis court and swimming pool.

The house wasn't new, but it showed evidence of having been remodeled to suit Obregon's taste. The exterior had been freshly painted and shiny new rain gutters fronted the eaves. The asphalt on the access road was also new, without a trace of the erosion it would show after one rainy season had passed.

Bolan hadn't used the road, but he had glimpsed it driving by and later when he walked back through the forest, moving parallel to keep himself on target. There were sentries covering the road, but he had managed to avoid them, focused as they were on watching out for men in vehicles.

He caught a break on booby traps, encountering none along the way, and reached his present vantage point unnoticed by the enemy. Decked out in forest camouflage, a nylon ski mask covering his face and war paint darkening his hands, he was invisible among the forest shadows.

Watching.

Bolan was a step ahead of Castillo that afternoon thanks to a friend of Brognola's at the DEA. The drug-enforcement people had Castillo covered, home and office, with a range of listening devices that enabled him to pick up phone calls, conversations in the flesh, and follow him from room to room. The Obregons had been more difficult to monitor, but when Castillo heard his master's voice "inviting" him to visit for a one-on-one, the word was passed along.

Eavesdropping on the conference was beyond Bolan's immediate capabilities, but he could keep the pressure on, keep rattling his enemies until they stumbled, made an irredeemable mistake.

His weapon for the penetration was a Steyr AUG assault rifle, chambered for the same 5.56 mm round as the American M-16 A-1. Another bullpup design, with its 30-round magazine mounted behind the trigger assembly, the AUG measured thirty-one inches overall and offered a cyclic-fire rate of 650 rounds per minute on full automatic.

The twenty-inch barrel came complete with a combination flash suppressor and grenade launcher. In addition to the bandolier of extra magazines across his chest, Bolan carried a shoulder-slung satchel of 40 mm MECAR rifle grenades, fired using normal ammunition, with a maximum effective range around one hundred meters.

Far enough to reach the manor house from where he was.

For close to half an hour he had scanned the grounds, observing sentries, noting patterns in their movements. Obregon took care with his security arrangements to a point, but there were also gaps. It would have cost a fortune to secure the woods around his home with cameras, sensors and listening devices. Francisco had the money, but he didn't bother, trusting in his hardforce to protect him.

The Executioner had counted fifteen men on duty, plus at least two more walkie-talkies on the access road. Assuming he had missed some, call it twenty guns, and that would be one shift. The same men couldn't be on duty around the clock. Twelve-hour shifts meant something close to forty guns in residence; eight-hour gigs would add another twenty men at least.

Where were they?

Studying the big house through the Steyr's optic sight, Bolan estimated thirty rooms at least. Assuming Obregon had any style at all, he wouldn't turn his lavish bachelor pad into a barracks for the troops, though some would certainly be quartered nearby to cope with any unforeseen emergencies. Behind the house he had already noted servants' quarters, plus a four-car garage with some kind of apartment on the second floor.

He estimated space for forty soldiers, tops. That meant a longer duty shift, perhaps reduced numbers at specified hours. It was probable, he realized, that the present show of force was unusual, provoked by his own hostile moves against Obregon in the past few hours.

For the first time since the Colombian landed in New Amsterdam, he had encountered opposition that he couldn't buy or frighten off.

The Executioner was watching when Castillo's limousine arrived. Bolan's pocket camera clicked off several photos for posterity before he stowed it and picked up the Steyr AUG.

Castillo needed time to get inside the house, meet Obregon, sit down, dispose of the amenities. If Bolan was correct in his assessment of the summons, little time would be consumed with small talk once the two had settled in. They had an unexpected shooting war to cope with, and the fact would soon be hammered home with even greater emphasis.

He lined up six grenades in front of him, a tidy row of minimissiles for the AUG, alternating HE and incendiary. Number seven, high explosive, was snapped onto the weapon's muzzle with a satisfying click.

All ready.

Bolan brought the weapon to his shoulder and peered through the optic sight, searching for a likely target.

"I THOUGHT YOU MIGHT HAVE some ideas or explanation for our recent difficulties," Francisco Obregon said. His tone was mild despite the firm set of his jaw.

"Unfortunately," Castillo replied, "I am at a loss. These incidents have been as much of a surprise to me as to yourself."

"And who do you suggest to be responsible?"

Castillo wriggled in his chair, distinctly ill at ease. "The only case for which I have an answer happened an hour ago at the New Market Mall. Gutierrez and some of his people were embarrassed by a Grandier campaign volunteer. It is unusual for one of them to show such spirit, but no one was killed. I have no reason to believe the incidents are related to your recent problem."

"*Our* problem," Obregon corrected him. "My men would not be here, would not be dying now, if it were not for my support of your campaign."

Castillo squirmed some more, eyes downcast, but Obregon suspected some of it at least had to be an act. The candidate was frightened—that was obvious—but he didn't believe he was in any major danger here at the estate. If anything, the house had to seem more like a sanctuary from the world outside.

Francisco was reminded of the reason why he hated politics and politicians. They were scheming liars, all of them, without the basic honor found in thieves and murderers. With an assassin, if he was a good one, you could pay your money, name the target and relax in the assurance that your hitter would perform as ordered, risking life and limb if necessary to achieve his goal. If he was captured, only the most foolhardy would ever name his sponsor to authorities, regardless of the danger to himself.

Given his opinion of politicians, plus Castillo's link to the Fidelistas in Havana, Obregon had entered their arrangement with his eyes wide open, guarding his back against any form of treachery. He was still on guard, but smooth sailing in New Amsterdam had admittedly caused him to relax in recent months, until the newest spate of violence shocked him back to full alertness. Now he had a war to fight, with no idea of who the enemy might be.

His own brother had narrowly escaped death, with three men shot down in his office during a sniper attack in broad daylight in downtown Hollandia. Who would attempt such a thing?

"You have your sources in the city," Obregon reminded his guest. "Can they tell you nothing?"

"So far, they claim total ignorance," Castillo answered. "I am pressing them, of course, but if the danger comes from outside..."

That brought Francisco's mind back to the States, where most of his cocaine was sold. Indictments waited for him there, and he would spend the rest of his life behind bars if the Americans ever got him in a courtroom. But these attacks were something else. His men had been killed in gangland style, albeit with unusual precision, and the nature of their deaths led Obregon to scan a mental list of enemies.

He was a bit surprised—and certainly relieved—to note that most of those he knew by name were dead, a few serving long terms in prison for various crimes. The few still left at large were widely scattered, hiding out in fear of their lives. They might cause trouble for Francisco in Colombia, given half a chance, but it was certainly beyond their capability to reach him in New Amsterdam.

Which left him with his pressing questions still unanswered.

"Fifteen men," he told Castillo. "It is unacceptable, you understand? Aside from the expense of their replacements, I cannot allow myself to be humiliated in this way."

"Of course, Francisco. I—"

Before Castillo had a chance to finish, he was interrupted by a loud explosion. Tremors rocked the house and glasses rattled on the shelf behind the wet bar on the far side of the study. Obregon lurched upright from his chair as members of his house staff shouted in the corridor outside.

A second blast followed close behind the first, erupting almost overhead. A rain of plaster dust fell down upon his desk, his hair, his shoulders.

Damn it all to hell!

Obregon saw Castillo moving toward him. He shoved the man aside and burst into the hallway, shouting orders to his men.

THE FIRST GRENADE SAILED through a ground-floor window at the northeast corner of the house and detonated with a muffled crash. An instant later smoke streamed from the shattered window. The yardmen were responding in a rush, none of them having spotted Bolan's sniper nest as yet.

Bolan mated a second grenade to the launcher, sighted through the Steyr's optic tube once more and picked a second-story window in the middle of the house, briefly checking the yard to make sure the nearest sentries were facing away from his lair when he fired.

This time the window was open, no resistance even from a pane of glass as the MECAR grenade spiraled through. Another crash, more smoke, and the warrior could well imagine what it felt like in the house about now, with dust and noise, Obregon's soldiers running back and forth in search of targets, anyone or anything on which to vent their sudden fear and rage.

He left them to it, primed a third grenade and swiveled to his left, toward the garage. The broad front doors were standing open, with shiny vehicles lined up inside. He picked a Jaguar, sandwiched in between a Porsche and a Mercedes, lining up his sights on the sports car's trunk.

The Jaguar went up like a king-size Molotov cocktail, flaming gasoline erupting from the ruptured fuel tank and spreading to the other cars. The Porsche caught fire before the Mercedes, but all of them were going, the classic restored Thunderbird last in line for a taste of cleansing fire.

Upstairs, in the apartment over the garage, Bolan caught a glimpse of frightened faces at the window. Flames spreading underneath their feet, they hit the stairs in shorts and socks, one man with time enough to get a shirt on, though he didn't button it. They reached ground level as the Thunderbird exploded, and a fireball swallowed both of them, stick figures thrashing in the midst of hell with blackened arms and legs.

Four grenades were left, but a couple of the yardmen had him spotted now, and Bolan knew that it was time to move, before they had a chance to find the range. He scooped up the remaining missiles in his left hand, backing into shadow as a short burst whispered overhead.

Bolan had the shooter spotted, and he swung the Steyr AUG in that direction, aiming the lightweight weapon like an oversize pistol. He stroked the trigger gently for a 3-round burst and watched his target stagger, going over backward in a lifeless sprawl.

Three other gunners raced toward him and he dropped one in midstride, the corpse sliding several yards across the grass, facedown, before it came to rest. The two survivors opened fire from forty yards and Bolan let the trees absorb their bullets, falling back to a secondary position. He would have to deal with them, and quickly, but he wouldn't let them choose the killing ground if he could help it.

Twenty yards made all the difference in the world. He found a shallow gully edged with ferns and ducked below the hunters' line of sight. Bolan waited, hearing them as they approached through the trees, all sound and fury, shouting back and forth to one another.

They came into view together, thirty feet between them, bracketing their target north and south. The gunner on the warrior's left was slightly closer, and he had a shotgun in his hands. He was therefore more likely to produce a hit than his companion, who held a shiny automatic pistol. Bolan chose his mark accordingly and swung the AUG hard left.

Four rounds cut loose with one stroke of the trigger and he saw the gunner's dress shirt ripple, crimson spouting from the wounds that clustered at his chest. The hardman vaulted over backward, losing his shotgun in the process, and was out of sight before his legs stopped twitching in their death throes.

His companion squeezed off three quick rounds, believing he had Bolan spotted, but the bullets whispered through the shrubbery somewhere off to the Executioner's right. It was a critical mistake in killing circumstances, and the gunner definitely wouldn't be permitted to correct his aim.

A burst of 5.56 mm tumblers effectively took him out of play.

Bolan still had four grenades, but they could wait for other targets, other times. He heard the numbers running in his head and knew that it would only qualify as senseless bravado to remain when Obregon's small army would be rapidly converging on him, cutting off retreat. The probe had never been designed as a decisive stroke, and it was time for the warrior to withdraw.

The gunners made it easy for him, milling on the lawn, some of them firing toward the trees without a clear-cut target, hanging back until they realized their comrades weren't coming out again. By the time one of Obregon's captains came out of the house and began to whip them into shape, Bolan had already slipped out of range. Before they started beating the brush in earnest, coming up empty, he was back at his car, changing out of the camo fatigues.

A fair start.

Driving back toward Hollandia, he thought Castillo and friends should be decently rattled by now, but Bolan wasn't backing off.

In fact, he was just getting started.

5

The speech had been arranged two weeks in advance, and Martin Grandier refused to cancel at the last minute, despite two attacks on his daughter in the space of seven hours. Alicia, likewise, wouldn't hear of it when her father tactfully suggested that she might stay home and listen to the speech on radio instead of turning out in person.

They were stubborn to a fault, these Grandiers, and Rafael Encizo knew that he was wasting time and breath when he attempted to dissuade them from a chosen course of action.

The alternative was to prepare himself as best he could for anything that might transpire. Encizo had no access to a firearm at the moment, but in the confusion following the melee at New Market Mall, he had been able to use a telephone in privacy and leave a message for Bolan at the cutout number they had prearranged. The brief advisory outlined what had happened since they separated, with a reminder of Grandier's scheduled address that evening in the heart of town.

At one point in the distant past, the present site of Exposition Park had been a public marketplace where everything from fruits and vegetables to human beings were sold. The slave trade had endured until the early nineteenth century, abolished by the government of Holland in the 1820s, and many of the liberated blacks stayed on, mingling their blood with the native islanders and, to a lesser extent, with the Dutch. The public marketplace had closed in 1958 and was replaced by Exposition Park, a combination landmark and memorial in the heart of modern Hollandia. Tradition reserved a part of the park for speeches by anyone with a cause to promote, and Martin Grandier was taking advantage of that fact with an appearance that would—he hoped—draw a crowd of several thousand curious observers.

Unless Encizo missed his guess, the turnout would include supporters of the opposition, willing—if they weren't actually under orders—to disrupt the meeting and discredit Grandier by any means available. Given the recent turn of events toward open violence, there was even a chance, however remote, that Castillo's DGI or Colombian backers might try to cinch the election by taking out Grandier altogether.

Encizo didn't waste his breath in trying to convince Alicia or her father they were making a mistake. Instead, he concentrated on the volunteers in charge of general logistics for the rally, studying their preparations with emphasis on security, riding along with Alicia to take a look at the park in advance of the gathering. He marked approach routes and potential exits in the case of an emergency, scanning nearby streets and giving up on coverage of potential sniper roosts among the high-rise buildings stacked on every side.

If trouble came, Encizo knew, it would be each man for himself.

And now the time had come. Encizo stuck close to Alicia as she covered final preparations for the rally, checking with the volunteers that would be stationed here and there throughout the crowd. Police were also on the scene, but Grandier had warned his people that the uniforms would only intervene if there was some major disturbance. Even then, they were as likely to arrest the victims as the aggressors, all in the name of "order."

In short, the party members would be on their own, reminded in advance of Grandier's commitment to nonviolence.

Encizo spent his time eavesdropping on Alicia's security precautions while he scanned the crowd for familiar faces. It was an exercise in futility, he realized, since he had met only four of the opposition so far, and three of those would be recuperating from their injuries that evening.

He watched out for their handler, though, the hulk Alicia had identified as one Ramon Gutierrez. At the same time, just in case, Encizo checked for random matches to the photos he had viewed at Stony Man Farm before departing from the States—the Obregons, a few of their ranking lieutenants, even Armand Castillo himself, though it would be insane for him to show his face in these surroundings.

Several hundred people were milling around the park when Encizo arrived, and he pegged the number at something over two thousand by the time Martin Grandier appeared. The tropical storm that had been threatening New Amsterdam wasn't supposed to strike before the next morning, and the crowd was obviously out to make the most of any time remaining.

Grandier's audience was a mixed bag in terms of gender, age and mode of dress. Encizo saw no elderly among them, but otherwise they ran the gamut from a handful of children to indeterminate middle age. None of those that he could see looked nervous, stressed or out of place. They might not all be sympathizers, but they didn't look like enemies.

Then again, you could never really tell.

He stuck close to Alicia, near the north end of the speaker's platform, only half listening as Martin Grandier was introduced. The speech meant nothing to Encizo, knowing as he did that any danger would be coming from the crowd or somewhere behind it.

He couldn't stop a sniper's bullet, no damned way at all, but if the enemy should come for Grandier at close range, they might have a fighting chance.

The Cuban settled in to wait.

RAMON GUTIERREZ recognized his enemy at a glance, despite the hundred yards and several hundred people between them. He was staring through binoculars, presenting the appearance of a Grandier supporter who was late arriving at the park and too reserved to push his way in closer to the dais. On his shirt, a plastic-coated button proclaimed Martin Grandier For A New Tomorrow In New Amsterdam.

Gutierrez had decreed that all his soldiers had to wear campaign buttons, ribbons and the like to mix in with the crowd. It was a flimsy ruse, but useful in the present circumstances. Grandier's campaigners wouldn't question total strangers bearing tokens of support. They were idealists, or so Gutierrez classified them, and idealists jumped at any evidence that gave them cause for optimism.

Three dozen handpicked thugs circulated through the crowd. Enough, in Gutierrez's opinion, to transform a group this size into a frantic mob. Any more would be too many, sluggers stumbling over one another, multiplying the inherent risk of capture by police. Three dozen, in a crowd of two-thousand-plus, could start a brawl and keep it rolling but slip away before the uniforms closed in.

And when they fled, they would be leaving at least one man dead.

Gutierrez didn't know the stranger's name, but he was gratified to see his face a second time. It had been painful, going to Armand Castillo with a bald report of failure in the simplest of tasks—three of his soldiers battered, needing treatment at the local hospital, defeated by a single man.

This time there would be no mistakes, no slipups. Gutierrez was supervising the kill himself, and he would join the action personally if he had to, get his own hands bloody one more time. As long as he wasn't identified or held for questioning, it would be pleasant, a treat to himself, relieving the frustration of his present circumstance.

Gutierrez wore a pistol in the waistband of his trousers, at the back. It was a Glock 23, chambered for the same .40-caliber Smith & Wesson cartridge lately favored by the American FBI, with thirteen rounds in the magazine and one in the chamber. He would use it if he had to, as a last resort, to wreak his vengeance on the enemy who had embarrassed him.

It would have pleased Gutierrez greatly to kill Martin Grandier at the same time, thus ensuring Castillo's victory, but his superiors within the DGI didn't want anything so obvious. External pressure was allowed, to rattle Grandier or even drive him from the race, but a direct assassination would reflect upon Castillo, possibly invite more meddling by the Dutch or even the Americans.

Gutierrez watched his target through the glasses, acting casual about it, flinching once when the stranger appeared to stare directly back at him. It was an illusion, of course. There was no way the man could pick him out this far away without field glasses of his own.

Already Gutierrez could see four of his soldiers in place, taking up their stations near the dais, ready to pounce on their man once the trouble got started. Ramon had pointed out the target in advance, making sure that his men understood their primary mission.

Search and destroy.

Gutierrez started to move closer, knowing the risks in advance, unwilling to trust his revenge to the hands of subordinates. The action at New Market Mall had taught Ramon a valuable lesson. Never again would he take a stranger or a victory for granted.

It was easy, moving toward the dais as the crowd closed in for a better view. Martin Grandier was on the stage now, flanked by campaign volunteers, his daughter still down in the audience with her high-kicking savior.

Good.

It would be better if they didn't have to go for him on the stage. There would be an opportunity when the fighting started. Who would notice when a knife slid home between the stranger's ribs? If it was done correctly, there would be no clue for the police to work from. Even if Gutierrez was forced to use the pistol, he was counting on the mob scene to protect him as he slipped away.

He had used the same technique before, in Nicaragua, where it had served him well. New Amsterdam would be no different if he kept his wits about him and didn't allow himself to make mistakes.

The mark of a professional.

ALICIA GRANDIER never tired of hearing her father speak. It was some kind of holdover from childhood, she realized, listening to him lecture before small local audiences, talking on the telephone to his reporters, sharing endearments with Alicia's mother before she had died, when Alicia was barely nine years old. From that time on her father's voice had been the touchstone of her life, extolling virtue as its own reward, cautioning tolerance of the unknown or unusual, ringing condemnation of bigotry in any form.

Despite the strain he had been facing during recent weeks, climaxed by the day's explosion of violence around Hollandia, he was still in good form. His voice was rich and mellow, even filtered through the bargain amplifiers they were using to reduce expenses.

Alicia listened to her father, but her eyes were on the crowd, watching for any sign of trouble in the upturned faces of the men and women pressing close around the dais. Her two brushes with disaster in the past ten hours had induced a state of mind approaching paranoia—with the difference that Alicia knew someone was out to harm her and would almost certainly repeat the effort sometime prior to the election.

Sometime soon.

She glanced at Raul Camacho, standing several yards away and to her right. He *was* attractive in a rugged sort of way. Not soft and weak like so many of the young men who were drawn to her father's campaign. She felt no personal disdain for the willing volunteers who kept the campaign rolling, but there was something about them—most of them, at any rate—that left her wishing for a *man*.

The thought surprised Alicia, almost made her blush. She turned back toward the dais, catching sight of Erno Soto on his folding chair behind her father. He was an example of the soft men that Alicia had in mind, and while he knew her father's ideology by heart, had gained his confidence and risen to the inner circle of the Independence Party, she could never help but think of him as toady.

It was irrational, Alicia realized. Soto and others like him were helping her father run against the special interests represented by Castillo. Without them, there would be no campaign to speak of, and it seemed churlish of her to dismiss them as weak, even effeminate. But she couldn't help her feelings, any more than she could divert the oncoming tropical storm by sheer force of will.

Perhaps it was her age, and the fact that she had yet to find the man Americans would christen "Mr. Right." She hadn't made an energetic search, by any means, convinced that love or its equivalent would find her when the time was right. But all her female friends from school were married now, or settled in careers that compensated on the surface for their lack of a relationship. She felt left out, to some degree—or, rather, left behind.

Raul Camacho might be "manly" in his way, but he was no fit prospect for commitment. He was an American, for one thing, bound to head back there when he was finished with his mission in New Amsterdam. On top of that, his life-style was abhorrent to the values she had learned while growing up. He was a man of violence, first and foremost, solving problems with his fists or any weapon he could reach in a pinch.

And still, she came back to the central fact—he was a *man.*

Alicia missed the trouble when it started, somewhere on the far left fringes of the crowd. A shoving match, with angry shouting, two men throwing punches, somehow missing each other, striking those around them. As the altercation spread, she heard the angry voices, felt a ripple starting in the close-packed crowd. Her father glanced in that direction, hesitating in the middle of a sentence, taking stock.

He was about to call for moderation when a second fight broke out, this one directly opposite the first, about sixty yards to Alicia's right. Instinctively she recognized the fact that it couldn't be a coincidence. Two brawls, "sponta-

neously'' breaking out at such a gathering, required at least
a modicum of orchestration, something in the nature of a
guiding hand.

Castillo.

Raul Camacho was moving toward her now, shoving
urgently past the spectators who stood between them,
keeping his eyes on the crowd at large. Alicia fought the
urge to run and waited for him where she was, somehow
confident that she had a better chance of escaping harm
with the Cuban-American at her side.

Her father was calling out for peace now, his speech
momentarily abandoned. On the far edge of the crowd, she
saw police uniforms closing in, black-gloved hands
wrapped around riot batons, clubs raised to strike. They
could have a full-scale riot on their hands in moments, she
realized, and what would happen then?

In front of her, two men began to quarrel, shoving each
other. Suddenly their fists were flying, and she saw a
crimson splash of blood from one man's nose. The mad-
ness was catching on, like some bizarre infection spread by
simple contact.

Alicia was retreating from the newest fight, a short step
backward, when a callused hand clamped tight across her
mouth, the stranger's other arm encircling her waist and
pinning both her arms at her sides.

ENCIZO RECOGNIZED a setup when he saw one, sluggers
planted in the crowd with orders to proceed on cue to get
the party rolling. Once the punches started landing, violence took on a life of its own, with total strangers caught
up in the fever to do something, anything, however wild or
irrational.

He fell back toward Alicia, recognizing from experience that she could be a target now that fighting had
erupted in the crowd. It was the perfect cover for a kidnapping or murder, and who could possibly remember
what became of one young woman in the middle of a riot?

Encizo picked up the first thug totally by instinct, closing on his right, a blur of motion with the knife held flat

against his thigh where it wouldn't cut anyone until he meant to strike, coming in like a pro, with his eyes focused strictly on his target.

Tunnel vision.

The little Cuban pretended not to notice him at first, checking for backup, spotting two other thugs bulling through the crowd on converging courses, cutting him off from three sides.

As casually as he could manage, Encizo checked his back, feeling a chill race down his spine at the sight of Alicia Grandier, wrapped in a no-neck gorilla's arms, being dragged toward the rear of the dais and out of the lights. No one on the stage appeared to notice, and Encizo knew that he had little time in which to help her.

First, though, he would have to help himself.

He felt the blade man step inside his circle, striking range. Encizo spun to face him, going underneath the thrust that should have slit his jugular, one arm extended with the fingers hooked like talons. He closed on the would-be killer's genitals and clamped down, Encizo's free arm rising to deflect the knife.

His claw hold bore immediate results. The blade man screamed and clamped his meaty thighs together, but the tactic only tightened Encizo's excruciating grip. His adversary's knees were folding, his free hand batting at Encizo's face without the necessary force to drive him back. It was no great trick to take the knife away from him, reverse the blade and attack.

The crimson rush was hot against the Phoenix Force warrior's knuckles, and the hitter looked surprised. His mouth dropped open, working silently, the new mouth underneath it spilling liquid life. He staggered backward as Encizo let him go, legs buckling, both hands coming up to try to close the six-inch gash that severed veins and arteries, his larynx—everything, in short, that he would need to stay alive for more than ninety seconds.

That left three, and Encizo was armed now, fading back toward where Alicia struggled with her captor, knowing that the other two would reach him before he had a chance to help the woman.

He was right. The squat gorilla on his left flank moved slightly faster than his comrade on the other side, attacking with an ice pick. They were obviously hoping for a silent kill, instead of simply peppering the crowd with gunfire.

As Ice Pick approached Encizo, he saw his comrade on the ground and hesitated for a moment, working up his anger for a rush that brought him in full-speed ahead, his pointy weapon held in front of him as if he were a jouster. Rafael stood firm and waited for him, stepping backward at the final instant and striking with his captured knife.

First stroke, he slit the veins and tendons in his adversary's outstretched wrist. Continuing without a break in motion, he performed a bit of sloppy surgery across one cheek, below the hitter's eye. Blood gouted from the wound and spattered on Encizo's shoes.

The Phoenix Force warrior followed through with a snap kick to the forehead, moving in behind the kick and stabbing twice beneath the big man's sternum.

Another gout of hot blood splashed on his wrist as the dead man folded and toppled forward on his face.

Encizo caught a glimpse of Alicia, slipping out of sight behind the dais now, but Number Three was coming for him in a rush before Encizo had a chance to brace himself. Instead of standing up to meet the charge, he pivoted and cocked his arm, releasing the knife in an overhand pitch from fifteen feet away.

Number Three could have saved himself, had he been lighter on his feet or less intent on covering the last few yards to make his kill and earn a bonus on the job. As it was, he met the twirling knife head-on, momentum adding to the impact, driving the blade even deeper into his chest.

He staggered, rocked back on his heels and dropped the razor he was carrying to reach up for the knife buried deep within a lung. It might not be a mortal wound, but it was good enough to take him out of action for the moment—all Encizo needed for his getaway.

In less than thirty seconds, he had caught up with Alicia and her captor, thankful for the slugger's single-minded concentration on the task at hand. Alicia's adversary had trusted his companions to eliminate Encizo while he dragged the woman to a nearby waiting car. He was entirely unprepared to feel strong fingers tangle in his hair and drag his head back at a choking angle, putting harsh strain on his vertebrae.

The slugger kept a tight grip on Alicia with his left hand even so, but he was fishing underneath his jacket with the right, going for hardware. Encizo caught his wrist and jerked it backward, putting pressure on until he felt the shoulder separate. The guy was cursing now, unable to maintain his crushing grip around Alicia's waist. Encizo had him on his knees, half-dazed with pain and momentarily defenseless.

It was no time for a sense of chivalry.

Encizo caught him with a swift kick to the face that snapped his head back and dumped him over backward in a silent sprawl. He might be dead or simply knocked unconscious. Either way, it made no difference to the Cuban. He had neutralized one threat, but there were clearly others circulating in the crowd.

He knelt beside the prostrate thug and reached inside his jacket, lifting out a Smith & Wesson Model 411 semiautomatic pistol. He could feel Alicia staring at him as he tucked the weapon in his waistband, turned toward her and reached for her arm.

"Let's go," he ordered, dragging her along beside him.

"But my father—"

"One thing at a time," he said, permitting her no room for argument. "Those goons were after us."

6

Erno Soto checked his own reflection in the rearview mirror of his Pinto, wincing as he stroked the bandage on his forehead with an index finger. Soto hated pain in any form, and even though the cut was minor, it distressed him.

There was nothing in the plan that called for him to be on the receiving end of any flying objects when the rally fell apart. He understood that it had been an accident—unplanned, at least, by those who paid his secret salary—but it was still unnerving.

Men had died at Exposition Park that very night, and when disruption turned to killing, Soto knew that anything could happen.

As for him, he didn't plan to make himself a target if he could avoid it. Pain was one thing; death was something else entirely. He had signed on as a spy within the Grandier campaign machine, and he had done his job extremely well so far. But it didn't include absorbing physical abuse, much less the risk of being killed by total strangers in a public park.

It would be difficult, but Soto meant to have a brief word with Ramon Gutierrez while they were together, make it clear that he wasn't a soldier or a thug. Gutierrez had no end of petty criminals on tap to do his dirty work. He didn't need Erno Soto in the front lines, having rocks bounced off his head.

The traitor left his car and locked it, careful of the neighborhood. There was a bar at each end of the street, loud music spilling from their open doors. The locals and a few of the more daring tourists would be belting drinks in preparation for the tropical storm that was supposed to strike New Amsterdam sometime the next day. If Soto knew the district—and he did—there would be several drunken fights inside the bars or on the streets before the block closed down an hour short of dawn.

So be it.

If Gutierrez scheduled meetings in a neighborhood where he felt most at home, that was his business. Soto merely had to keep the date, report and register his personal objection to the violence he had suffered.

In between the bars, a string of shops had shut down for the night, their doors and windows mostly darkened, several screened by bars or shutters that would disappear in daylight, when the tourists in their garish flowered shirts came out to throw their cash around as if there was no tomorrow.

No tomorrow.

Soto had a new feel for the phrase this evening, after Exposition Park. He knew the absence of a future could be literal instead of figurative. Men were dying in the campaign now, and Soto didn't plan to be one of them.

A match flared in the doorway opposite his car, illuminating Gutierrez's face for an instant. Soto made his way across the street, checking each direction for spies instead of traffic, spotting no one who could give his double-dealing game away. He stepped into the shadows, smelling the Cuban's cheap cigarette and the discount cologne he sometimes used in lieu of bathing.

"What went wrong?" Gutierrez asked without so much as a passing nod to the amenities.

"You're asking me?" Soto didn't have to feign his dismay. "A rock came flying out of nowhere and it hit me in the face. It could as easily have been a bullet. I didn't agree—"

"An accident," Gutierrez interrupted him, dismissing the complaint. "I want to know what happened with the woman."

"How should I know?" Soto countered, feeling anger warm his cheeks and knowing it was dangerous. He made a conscious effort to relax as he continued. "One of your men grabbed her from behind. I saw that much. He pulled her back behind the stage. I wasn't told to follow them and didn't have the chance, in any case."

Again he gestured to the bandage on his forehead, hoping it would make a difference, earn some sympathy. Gutierrez either didn't notice or didn't care.

"Three of my men were killed tonight," he said. "A fourth is in the hospital. Intensive care. He may not live. The man who did this has escaped me for a second time. You understand that I am not concerned about a scratch you got while running for the sidelines, Erno?"

As he spoke, Gutierrez reached out and prodded Soto's bandage, sending jolts of pain through his skull. Soto recoiled from the larger man's touch but restrained an urge to slap his hand away.

"I understand," he muttered, glowering.

"You're paid to be my eyes inside the Grandier campaign," Gutierrez went on. "I need to find the woman. Are we clear on this?"

"She hasn't called her father since the rally," Soto answered. "Also missing is a new man on the team. A volunteer, Raul Camacho. It is possible they slipped away together. No one knows where they have gone."

"Describe this new man," Gutierrez snapped.

Soto did as he was told, watching the Cuban's face mold itself into a mask of anger as he spoke. When he was finished, Gutierrez took a last draw on his cigarette and flicked it into the street.

"I want to know immediately when they surface, night or day. You understand me, Erno? This is critical. You must not fail in this."

The traitor nodded, understanding perfectly.

He understood that he had graduated from the spying game to something more extreme. His life was riding on the line, and there was nothing he could do about it now but follow orders, hoping for the best.

With any luck at all, he just might save himself.

THE SMALL APARTMENT was a fallback option, rented in advance when Stony Man was laying groundwork for the action in New Amsterdam. The place came furnished with the bare essentials, doubtless purchased from Hollandia's equivalent of Wal-Mart, but the plumbing worked, it had a telephone, and the absentee landlord obviously didn't give a damn what happened underneath his roof, as long as he was paid on time and no one set the place on fire.

Alicia Grandier, though shaken by the violence in the park, had still recovered far enough to look askance at her surroundings once Encizo closed and locked the door.

"You're living here?" she asked.

"Not really. It's a bolt hole."

"Pardon?"

"Like a safehouse," Encizo explained. "A place to hide."

"You have a need of hiding places in your line of work?"

"From time to time," he said. "It seems that you do, too."

She checked out the sofa, as if the dingy color of its fabric might rub off and stain her clothes, but finally she sat. The expression on her face was stuck somewhere between depression and fatigue.

"You killed those men back there," she said at last. "There must have been some other way."

"Of course. I could have let them murder me and kidnap you. It struck me as a bad idea, but if you'd rather be with them right now, I'm sure they have men looking for you all around Hollandia."

She thought about that for a moment, then softened. "I'm sorry. That was churlish of me. Three times you have saved my life, and I complain about your methods. Still..."

"I understand. You don't believe in violence, regardless of the cause."

"That's not entirely true," Alicia said. "I recognize the concept of a just war, self-defense, that sort of thing. But everything that happens in regard to the political campaign reflects upon my father. You can see that, surely."

"That's the plan," Encizo replied. "Castillo's people didn't start that riot in the hope of making headlines for themselves. They want to smear your father—and, while they're about it, take you hostage. My best guess would be that they're counting on a plea from you to make your father quit the race."

"I'd never ask that of him."

Encizo sat beside her on the couch, a foot or so of empty air between them. "I suspect you wouldn't have to," he replied. "Castillo's people know exactly what to say, what threats to make. They'd let you live just long enough to make a phone call and confirm they had you in the bag. It wouldn't matter what you said. Unless I'm very wrong about your father, he would drop the race to save your life."

"You're right, of course." Her eyes were brimming now—with tears of sadness or delayed reaction to the fight at Exposition Park, he couldn't tell.

"Which is exactly why we need to keep you under wraps," Encizo said. "The more you make yourself available, the easier you make it for your father's enemies to do their job."

"I can't just hide for two whole weeks."

"Twelve days," he carefully corrected her. "And it won't be that long. I have a feeling things are due to change within the next few hours."

"Change? What do you mean?"

"I really can't go into that," he told her.

"Can't or won't?"

"It cuts both ways. Your father has me isolated from my friend, which means my flow of information is extremely limited right now. The things I do know, I can promise you, you wouldn't want to hear."

"It doesn't matter what I want," Alicia said. "Before this morning, I had never seen a person killed. Dead bodies, yes, but not the act itself. Today I've averaged close to one an hour since breakfast. Are you telling me there's worse to come?"

"I'm telling you the tables have been turned against Castillo and his goons. He doesn't know it yet, but he's about to get the message."

"From your friend?"

"From people who would rather see New Amsterdam elect a leader than a puppet owned by Castro or the Medellín cartel."

Alicia changed the subject, catching Encizo off guard. "I haven't thanked you properly."

"It isn't necessary."

"I believe it is." She leaned in closer to him as she spoke, the invitation unmistakable.

Her lips were soft and warm, first hesitant, then parting at one first touch of his tongue. Encizo felt warmth spreading through his loins, a loud alarm bell sounding in his mind before he switched it off.

There was no sense of a commitment here on either side. It was a sharing, a release, entirely mutual, with no demands or expectations held on either side. An inner voice urged him to go for it, to let the moment be.

Encizo let himself relax and feel the heat.

THE RIOT in Exposition Park led news broadcasts throughout the evening in Hollandia, and while each of several reporters tried to put a new twist on the story, their reports were much the same. Two dozen people were injured, one of them in critical condition from a beating. Three men were stabbed or slashed to death, and the authorities were questioning Martin Grandier.

Mack Bolan didn't have to stop in at the morgue before he made an educated guess as to the general affiliation of the three fatalities. If they were Grandier campaigners, every news hawk in the capital would be reporting it by now. The very fact that they were unidentified told Bolan one of two things: either none was carrying ID, or the police were working overtime to trace their possible complicity in the explosive violence in the park.

Whichever way he read it, though, the message was the same—Castillo's thugs had come up short again, and three of them had paid for the mistake in blood.

He knew from a message on the answering machine that served their cutout line that Rafael Encizo had been present at the rally. Bolan had considered stopping by to watch the action, but he trusted Encizo to cope with any problems that arose, and there was other work for him to do around Hollandia.

The bombs, for instance, had been planted more for nuisance value than for any telling impact they would have on business for the Obregons. He'd targeted a smallish fleet of trucks sequestered in the parking lot behind a warehouse, ringed by chain-link fence. There was no voltage in the wire, and no alarm to bring the sentries running as he cut a gateway for himself and made his way inside.

The packets were incendiary, with just enough plastique to get the bonfire rolling and ensure some crippling damage—twelve trucks, six bombs. A matter of economy. The six that blew would bathe the other six in blazing fuel.

The warrior was a block away before the timers ran down together, the explosions lighting up the warehouse parking lot as bright as day. He stood and watched the trucks as they were shattered and devoured by flames, stick figures scampering around the fringes of the conflagration, shouting questions and instructions. All in vain.

A small thing, but it kept the enemy off guard.

The Obregons were thinking of him even now. They didn't know his face or name, had no idea of where he came from or his motives for attacking them, but Bolan knew that he was on their minds.

Psy War.

It was among the oldest strategies of human conflict, even though the name kept changing with successive generations. Terrorists were masters of the concept, understanding that an enemy confused and frightened was an enemy half-beaten. You could break a man—inside his head—before you ever met him face-to-face.

The Obregons weren't that soft, of course, with years of double-dealing and assassinations in the cocaine trade behind them, but they weren't immune to human doubts and feelings, either. Paranoia was a built-in factor of their chosen trade. All dealers watched their backs incessantly, alert to any danger from police, competitors, their own employees setting up a move to bump the present ruler from his roost.

It was a combination of survival mechanism and inherent weakness, something Bolan knew that he should take advantage of and use against his adversaries. Ideally the warrior would have liked to play one drug gang off against another, but the Obregons appeared to hold a functional monopoly. Still, there were Cuban activists involved, and Armand Castillo with his own ambitions to be satisfied.

The possibilities weren't exactly endless, but they were enough for Bolan's needs. He merely had to seize the opportunities as they arose and turn them to his own advantage, making sure that he did not wind up as a statistic in the process.

What next?

He ran the mental list of targets, correlating recent information from Brognola's contact in the DEA. New Amsterdam was still wide open to the Executioner, with targets readily available. He merely had to pick one and make his move.

WHEN THE POLICE were finished with him, Martin Grandier allowed his bodyguards to drive him home. He had intended to revisit Exposition Park, but the interrogation left him feeling drained, exhausted, desperate for some peace and quiet. There was nothing he could do for those who had been injured in the riot, much less for the three men who had died.

As for Alicia, Grandier had been relieved to hear that she was safe and sound. At first he was afraid she had been kidnapped, but her call to campaign headquarters, relayed by Erno Soto, put his mind at ease. Raul Camacho had preserved her safety for the second time that day, and while her whereabouts were still unknown—she had refused to say where she was hiding, for the moment—Grandier drew solace from the very fact that she hadn't been harmed.

The same couldn't be said for his campaign.

He had no doubt that the police investigation would exonerate his volunteers, but the report would almost certainly come after the election. Government officials in New Amsterdam were no more speedy or efficient than their counterparts in London, Moscow or Washington. They took their own sweet time, and if the delay made Grandier look guilty in the meantime, well, it would all be explained in the end.

Too late.

He had no doubt that it was part and parcel of Armand Castillo's strategy to make it seem that Grandier had lost control of his campaign, his followers. An incident like the one in Exposition Park was worth a thousand votes for Grandier's opponent on election day, if it was properly exploited.

Castillo had no problems in that regard, Grandier knew. His publicity machine was second to none, amply funded by contributions from his silent partners in the campaign. Drug money, for the most part, though Grandier couldn't prove it. Perhaps some cash from Cuban Communists, as well, if the Americans were being truthful for a change.

By morning, news of the events in Exposition Park would have spread from Hollandia throughout the land, on from there to the United States. It would certainly make front-page news in Amsterdam, and while the present government of the Netherlands had promised to refrain from intervention in the ongoing campaign, the slanted reports would mean a black eye for Martin Grandier.

At heart, the candidate was less concerned with his own reputation than with what a defeat at the polls would mean for his country. Grandier feared Armand Castillo, not so much for what the man could order done to him or even to Alicia, but for the effect that he would have upon New Amsterdam as the prime minister. Already he corrupted those around him at the slightest opportunity, and he was still a private citizen. As the prime minister, Castillo would be in position to subvert whole agencies and turn them into adjuncts of his own corrupt machine. Through bribes and patronage appointments, he could stack the government with sympathizers, frustrate law enforcement, introduce new legislation tailored by and for his covert allies.

It would be disaster for New Amsterdam, and while Grandier didn't envision himself as any kind of savior, he understood that no one else was ready at the moment to oppose Castillo's plan. If he was beaten on election day, it would be six long years before an honest man had any chance at all to seize the reins of government. By that time, with Castillo at the helm, it might well be too late.

The candidate made no objection when he noted that his bodyguards were wearing guns. A few of them were always armed, out of concern for Grandier's safety, and he had managed to ignore it in the past. Now, in light of the recent violence directed at his volunteers in general and Alicia in particular, he realized that some form of defense was necessary.

He couldn't defeat Armand Castillo from the grave.

That understanding didn't mean that Grandier was giving up his principles, by any means. He wasn't going over to the plan espoused by Mike Belasko and his sidekick, even though the two men had been instrumental in saving Grandier's daughter from abduction and almost certain death. Defense was one thing: terrorism was another.

Even in a world where violence seemed inescapable, it could be limited and channeled. It would never be constructive, in the strictest sense, but men could still restrain their more chaotic and destructive urges, fighting only when their lives and families were threatened or the future of their nation might be hanging in the balance.

Grandier would do his fighting at the lectern and the ballot box, whenever possible, but he wasn't about to let his hopes and his campaign go up in smoke without a strong show of resistance.

It wasn't too late; he wouldn't let it be too late.

They still had almost two weeks left before election day, and Grandier would give it everything he had, down to the wire. If that meant risking life and limb, so be it. He had placed his body on the line before for lesser issues, and he had survived.

Fat drops of rain were spattering the windshield by the time they reached his house. They were still few and far between, but he had followed the reported progress of the storm as it approached New Amsterdam. A few more hours, and the wrath of nature would be loosed upon his island home.

A sign, perhaps?

Martin Grandier wasn't a religious man. Any faith left over from his childhood had been swept away by the untimely death of his beloved wife. If Grandier was forced to choose a personal religion now, he would have gone for deism—the view that a Creator might exist, but that He lost all interest in His creatures once the novelty of forming them had passed.

The candidate had seen too much of poverty, corruption, misery and pain to put his trust in supernatural solutions. Man alone had turned the world into a kind of living hell, and only man could sort out the problems.

Assuming he had time.

New Amsterdam could be a start, but not if honest men of goodwill turned their backs on reason and abandoned their convictions out of fear.

The race was far from over.

It would take more than scattered raindrops and the threats of violent men to divert Martin Grandier from his destiny.

"Inside," he told his bodyguards in a tone that brooked no argument. "We must examine what there is to salvage from this night."

7

Emilio Guzman had never been fond of traveling by sea. His stomach always let him down, in spite of different medicines he took to quell the roiling, sour feeling that inevitably left him kneeling in the head, his last meal swirling in the toilet bowl.

It was a joke to those he sailed with, even though they kept it to themselves. Guzman's reputation made it dangerous for anyone to laugh at his expense, but he could tell what they were thinking when they watched him stagger up on deck. It didn't bother him to kill a man—or a woman, for that matter—but let him feel the rocking motion of a boat beneath his feet, and he was beaten.

What would happen, Guzman sometimes wondered to himself, if they were set upon at sea by enemies, hijackers or police? Could he do his duty? Would the rumbling in his gut prevent his taking aim and squeezing off a kill shot?

He knew that Pablo Obregon had to trust him, or he wouldn't be included every time a shipment sailed from Punta de Gallinas. Most of the cocaine traffic was shipped by air, but some deliveries went out through surface traffic to confuse the DEA. The high-tech yachts could almost sail themselves, which left the crew more time for dealing with security.

Emilio Guzman was a triggerman from Medellín. He knew that he would never rise to manage the cartel, and he was satisfied with his position in the world. It paid him well enough to meet his needs, with cash to spare, and there were always women for the taking. More important, he enjoyed his work. There was a rush that came with

killing, all that power funneled through his hands, hi
weapon, reaching out to claim another's life.

It made Guzman feel like God.

There had been no call for his special talents on this tri
so far, and at the moment he was simply feeling ill.]
wasn't quite so bad when they were docked, the *Corazó*
de Oro tied up fore and aft, but he was still aware of shift
ing water underneath the keel, enough to upset his stom
ach as he leaned against the rail.

He couldn't go ashore until the merchandise was trans
ferred, at which time he was expected to accompany th
shipment as a guard. Until the pickup, he was stuck o
board the yacht with the sensation in his belly, wishing h
could find some magic charm to make it go away.

There had been trouble in New Amsterdam, Guzma
understood, although he didn't know the details. Severa
men, including friends of his, had lost their lives. H
would enjoy repaying their killers in kind, if given half
chance.

But first he had the shipment to consider. Nothing too
priority over the smooth flow of merchandise and cash
Guzman's one and only duty with the Medellín cartel wa
taking care of business.

At the moment he was technically on guard. He didn'
for a moment think that there was any danger to the mer
chandise on board the yacht, but one could never be en
tirely certain. Cocaine could attract some maniacs, th
kind of man who took a dozen bullets standing on his fee
and cursed you with his dying breath before he hit th
floor.

Guzman's kind of man.

How many had he killed in fourteen years of serving th
cartel? The first three years or so, he had kept track of th
numbers in a little notebook that he carried, placing smal
stars on a calendar at home, much like a schoolboy wit
his homework. Keeping count. From that point on, the
started piling up, and Guzman had grown tired of num
bers. Style was more important, after all, enjoying wha
you did and making damned sure that you did it bette

than the next man. Keep on top of things and never take a back seat to the opposition, even if you had to risk your life.

The rep was everything in Guzman's line of work. You earned a name by demonstrating your ferocity and kept it up by periodic exhibitions, letting everybody know up front that you weren't a punk or easy mark.

No one mistook Emilio Guzman for a punk these days. His reputation would be good for years, even if he should never pull another trigger in the line of duty.

But he liked killing. It was one thing in the crazy world that gave him satisfaction.

His mind was on the shifting motion of the deck beneath his feet, the sound of water lapping up against the hull. He nearly missed the slightly different sound that emanated from behind him, and it took a heartbeat for his mind to register exactly what was different about the sound.

It was a dripping noise, like water falling on the deck, and something like the soft tread of a footprint. Almost like—

A strong hand caught him by the chin and twisted, cutting off the possibility of any sound escaping his throat. He felt the cold blade pierce his neck below the baseline of his skull, blazing white hot as it penetrated the aperture known among ancient Chinese as the wind gate, seeking his brain.

Following a rapid stirring motion of the killer's knife hand, Guzman went as limp as dirty laundry in his arms. Another moment, and the gunner's body slipped across the rail headfirst and disappeared beneath the surface of the water he had hated so in life.

IT WASN'T EVEN SWIMMING, really, when you thought about it. Bolan simply eased himself into the water fifty yards downrange and worked his way along the dock, hand over hand, until he reached the *Corazón de Oro*.

Heart of Gold.

It wasn't bad as names went, but it positively reeked when Bolan thought about the great yacht's cargo and the men on board who made their living from the misery and death of others. There wasn't a golden heart among them—few would even qualify as human, if you thought for any length of time about their crimes—and they were all fair game in the Executioner's war.

Before he went aboard the yacht, he fixed a squat magnetic charge against her hull, below the waterline. The timer gave him ten full minutes, more than he should need, with any luck at all.

The sentry on the deck was tall for a Colombian, but he wasn't on full alert. It seemed he almost noticed Bolan at the final instant, when it was too late to save himself. The muffled splash of his body slipping into the ocean didn't rouse his comrades in the pilothouse.

Bolan returned the fighting knife to its sheath, then opened the waterproof pouch at his waist and extracted the Beretta 93-R, with its 20-round magazine and customized silencer. He had the weapon set for semiautomatic fire, holding the option of 3-round automatic bursts in reserve for a special emergency, aware that traveling light meant only two spare magazines before he had to fall back on the knife and grapple with his opposition hand-to-hand.

Still, that was sixty rounds, and there should be no more than ten or fifteen men on board. If some of them had gone ashore already, that would shave the odds.

It would have been a simple thing to let the underwater charge do all the work, risk losing some of Obregon's commandos in the knowledge that the yacht and the cargo of cocaine would surely be destroyed. But that had never been Bolan's way.

He saw no point in taking on a job if he didn't intend to do it properly.

One minute seven seconds had elapsed as Bolan circled toward the pilothouse with the Beretta in his fist. The captain of the yacht was lounging in a sturdy, padded chair, two crewmen slouched in front of him, both smiling at the story he was telling. They glanced at the doorway as the Executioner rushed through it, immediately losing their smiles at the sight of his pistol.

He didn't wait for any of the three to reach a weapon. Everyone aboard the yacht was Bolan's enemy, each one involved in smuggling cocaine. They were condemned by circumstance, their choice of a career, and he wasn't their judge.

He was their judgment.

The warrior shot the standing crewmen first, a quick one-two that punched them over backward almost simultaneously, dumping them on the deck. The captain swiveled toward him with a dazed expression on his face, jaws working silently, and Bolan put a parabellum round between the twitching lips. Explosive decompression blew the captain's hat off, dropped it on the nearest crewman's chest, while crimson streamers dribbled from the window at his back.

Four down.

Emerging from the pilothouse, he met another crewman coming from below decks. The sailor was whistling, but choked on the tune as Bolan stepped in front of him and shot him in the face.

And that made five.

Four others sat around a table in the mess, one sipping coffee while the other three drank beer. The coffee drinker saw him coming down the companionway and dropped his mug, the steaming liquid sloshing in his lap. A shout of pain and warning made it out before a parabellum mangler drilled his forehead, silencing his voice forever.

Bolan worked his way around the table, firing on the move to pin the shooters down and so eliminate their threat. The last man, sitting with his back to the warrior, managed to extract a pistol from his waistband. He twisted in his chair to aim and fire, but all in vain. A hot 9 mm double punch ripped through his jaw and throat, sheared through his spine and dumped the flaccid rag-doll figure backward on the floor.

Evacuating, Bolan reached the afterdeck with three full minutes left. He used part of it to stow the 93-R in its watertight protective pouch, then threw himself across the rail, feet first into the water with a shallow splash.

He covered thirty yards with long, fierce strokes and scrambled from the water to the dock a few yards from the point where he had left his clothes. It was important that he clear the water well before the charge went off, to save himself from injury.

The *Corazón de Oro* might not have a heart of gold, but in another moment Bolan saw its heart of fire. A geyser marked the point of underwater detonation, followed swiftly by a red-orange ball of flame that leaped up from below decks, blossomed on the deck and shredded into tatters in the air. The shock wave sent a ripple through the pier, and he could feel reflected heat against his skin from where he stood.

It was time to leave, without watching the boat slip away. It was going, and that was what counted.

The Executioner had to move on to the next target.

AT TIMES LIKE THESE Ruud Manders wondered why he had selected diplomatic service as a personal career. He could have been a civil servant, putting in his time on simple paperwork, advancing up the ladder of seniority, untouchable unless they caught him stealing petty cash.

It had been the lure of glory, Manders decided, or something in his nature that had driven him to pursue a life outside the plodding mainstream, searching all his days for... what?

Adventure? Romance? Fame and fortune?

There had been a bit of each in his career, of course, but he was pushing sixty-five now, mandatory retirement age for political appointees, and New Amsterdam would be his final posting. Sadly it would also be his worst, and Manders was afraid of going home to Arnhem with this blot on an otherwise distinguished record.

Still, there seemed to be no action he could take that would alleviate the situation. His superiors had no desire for a solution, short of granting independence and allowing the infernal natives to thrash the rest out for themselves. That was the whole point of Manders's appointment, after all. He was a caretaker, nothing more or less, a figurehead to occupy the seat of government these last few days, before the whole thing went to hell.

It might not be that bad, of course. He knew both candidates and thought that either man was capable of picking up the reins, if he was willing to accept advice from someone with a bit of practical experience. Castillo had some problems with his background, Manders knew, and he was running with associates that raised some eyebrows back in Amsterdam. But that was politics. It made strange bedfellows, and no mistake.

As for the newsman, Grandier, he was described by all who knew him as a scrupulously honest man. Unfortunately that didn't equate to automatic aptitude for politics—some would suggest it meant the very opposite—but Grandier had been observing and reporting on the government for long enough to understand its workings, at the very least. And no one could suggest that he was short on theories or ideals.

It had been an interesting race, until the violence started. Nothing serious at first, a fistfight now and then between the overzealous volunteers of separate camps, but now the pace had escalated. There was brawling in the streets, combatants resorting to lethal weapons. Men were dying.

And Ruud Manders was responsible, at least on paper, for the maintenance of order through election day.

As the last colonial governor of New Amsterdam, he was required to see that laws were duly carried out, enforced, obeyed. He had police at his disposal, plus a military force of eighty men that he could mobilize in an emergency if he consulted his superiors beforehand. The police were trained, and they had weapons specially designed for dealing with disorder in the streets.

The problem, Manders knew, lay in his *other* duty. His unwritten, unrecorded orders from the men who mattered had already relegated Manders to the role of an observer in Hollandia, reduced to watching the election run its course. It was decreed that no one with a link to the colonial regime could be discovered meddling in the campaign. The world was watching, in between diversions from the hot spots of the globe, and no one in authority was anxious to be charged with having managed the election.

Manders understood that there was also some degree of spite involved. New Amsterdam had been a problem for the Netherlands of late. Tourism didn't pay the bills at home, the natives had complained about their status as a colony, and lately the Americans had been protesting the narcotic traffic through Hollandia. It was a simple answer to unload the island, let the natives have their way— and if they wound up looking foolish in the bargain, why, so much the better. Veteran diplomats would nod, smile knowingly, exchanging comments on the plight of simple men who pushed too far, too fast.

And if the whole thing went to hell once Manders and his people had withdrawn, well, that was simply one more piece of evidence that they were right to leave.

Still, he hated to see it end this way. It felt . . . wrong. There should be something he could do about the mayhem in the streets, if nothing else. While he was thinking, Manders poured himself another double Scotch whisky and settled in behind his massive desk.

THE PHONE CALL TOOK Francisco Obregon completely by surprise. He had been following the action in Hollandia and elsewhere, toting up the dead, dismayed to find that nearly all of them were his. Castillo's man, Gutierrez, had lost three at Exposition Park—perhaps a fourth, if they got sloppy in intensive care—but all the rest were Obregon's, cut down by enemies he couldn't name. Run out of his own house, goddammit, and forced into second-class quarters while he was waiting for something to break.

And now the yacht had been sunk. More men and close to thirty million dollars' worth of merchandise had been destroyed in the explosion. Obregon was fuming when the phone rang. His houseman took it, mumbled briefly to the caller, then finally approached his boss with a hesitant expression on his face.

"Some man says he has to talk to you about the boat."

"Who is it?"

"I don't know. He wouldn't give his name. You want me to hang up?"

Obregon thought about it, then finally shook his head. "I'll take it to find out what this guy has to say."

His houseman brought the cordless phone and closed the door behind him as he left.

"Who is this?"

"Names aren't important." There was subtle power in the voice, a confidence Francisco recognized at once.

This man was dangerous.

"Okay, then." He tried a different approach. "What do you want?"

"I thought I'd give you some advice," the stranger said. "New Amsterdam is heating up. You hang around much longer, I can guarantee you're going to get burned."

Obregon stiffened, feeling anger warm his cheeks. "You got this number and asked for me by name. You must know who you're talking to."

"That's right."

"You don't need any kind of balls to threaten people on the phone, okay? You want to meet me somewhere, we can talk about it, maybe sort things out."

"We met already, more or less," the caller said. "I did a little touch-up on your house this afternoon. Before that, I dropped by your brother's office. How's he doing, by the way?"

"He's doing fine."

"He needs to watch those picture windows," the stranger warned. "Too much sun can kill you."

"What's your point?"

"I like boats, too. You had a nice one down at the marina, didn't you?"

Obregon's knuckles whitened from clutching the receiver in a death grip. "Who the hell are you?"

"What's happened to my manners? All this time and I didn't introduce myself." There was a hint of laughter in the stranger's voice. "I'm your worst nightmare come to life, Francisco. How's that sound?"

"It sounds to me like you've got tired of living. Maybe lost your mind."

"We're all on borrowed time, Francisco. Think about it. I can hear the stopwatch ticking. You're a little short."

"And that's supposed to scare me? Big talk from a man who doesn't even show his face."

"You want to see my face," the stranger said, "just keep looking over your shoulder. I'll be the one breathing down your neck, setting your shirttail on fire."

"You haven't done your homework, man, if you think I scare that easy."

"I don't want to scare you. I'm just telling you that the only chance you have to save yourself right now is to pack your soldiers up and catch the next flight off New Amsterdam. I don't care where you go, as long as it's one way."

"I'm supposed to walk out just like that?" Despite his anger, it was all that Obregon could do to keep from laughing at the stranger's arrogance.

"Your choice," the caller said. "If you don't like walking out, I'm sure the state can find someone to carry you and stick your casket on a plane."

"Big talk. If you were standing here, I'd cut your throat and pull your tongue out through the hole, you hear me?"

"Loud and clear, Francisco. I'm just wondering how good you are without an army at your back. You've lost—what is it?—forty, forty-five percent of your original support team. The survivors must be getting nervous, even if it doesn't show right now. Too bad for you if they start to fade away and leave you flat."

"Nobody's leaving me!" Francisco blurted, feeling suddenly embarrassed that this total stranger had managed to put him on the defensive. "Pick the time and place if you want to find out what I've got."

"I'll do that. In the meantime, you keep counting heads. And watch your back."

"I'll watch you scream your fucking life away, you—"

He was talking to the dial tone, cursing as he flung the cordless telephone across the room. It struck a padded easy chair, rebounding to the carpet. Silence closed in around Francisco as he stood there, trembling with rage.

The voice had been American, of that he had no doubt. But what did that mean in the greater scheme of things? What did it say about his enemy, the best way to defeat him?

Obregon wasn't defeated yet, nor would he be defeated by a stranger babbling on the telephone.

It was time for Medellín to take the offensive.

Starting now.

8

The call from Stony Man had come in twenty minutes earlier while Bolan was engaged in baiting Obregon. He checked the cutout number, beeped the answering machine and listened to the cryptic message waiting for him there.

A woman's voice announced the date and time, then she instructed, "Striker, call the Farm, ASAP. Repeat, ASAP."

That made it urgent, and he used the cutout number's other function, calling back from what appeared to be a residential line, avoiding any hassle with an operator over small change on the pay phone. Twenty minutes wasn't that much leg time for a message from the States. An hour would have been acceptable in normal circumstances, but he didn't want to take the chance.

ASAP.

As soon as possible.

A steady drizzling rain was falling on the phone booth as he made his call and waited, listening to hollow sounds on the long-distance line. It took some time, despite the fact that he had dialed direct, before he heard Aaron Kurtzman's deep, familiar voice.

"Hello?"

"Hello, Bear. Striker checking in."

Relief was audible in Kurtzman's voice. "Are you secure?"

"We're on the cutout. No one's tumbled to it yet, as far as I can tell."

"You haven't got a scrambler handy?"

"No."

"Okay, then. Here's the scoop. You've got some company arriving from Havana pretty soon. A DGI contingent coming in to help their candidate. They get the news in Cuba, too, I guess. You shook them up the past few hours."

"Good."

"As long as they don't take you by surprise."

"You have arrival information?" Bolan asked.

"Affirmative." He listened, memorizing details and repeating them for confirmation when Kurtzman was finished—the arrival time, flight number, with an estimated head count for the Cuban team.

Six men would arrive, and what would they be hoping to accomplish with a force that size?

"It isn't much," he said to Kurtzman.

"Doesn't have to be," the Bear replied. "They're officers, from what I understand. Some kind of oversight committee. Could be that Fidel is having second thoughts about your buddy being man enough to run the show."

"It's late to think of changing horses," Bolan said.

"Agreed, but these boys may be packing spurs. Get things on track would be their angle, I suspect. You've got a bunch of Cubans on the scene already. All they need is some direction."

"I suppose the new kids on the block could stand a welcome."

"Couldn't hurt. We're leaving that to your discretion, naturally."

The Executioner couldn't resist a smile at that. "I'll see what I can do."

"Received and registered," Kurtzman replied. "I'll pass it on."

"That's it, then?"

"For the moment. You stay frosty, hear?"

"Down to the bone."

He cradled the receiver and put the booth behind him, moving through the steady drizzle toward the rental car. He had an hour and a half to go before the next Cubana

Airlines flight touched down and brought the Fidelistas to Hollandia. Before that happened, he would have to get in touch with Rafael Encizo and arrange the welcome party Stony Man was counting on.

A little something special for the DGI.

He had already seen the airport, southeast of town. Security was average, nothing a determined warrior couldn' circumvent if he tried.

He thought about the odds, the body count so far, and knew the war was escalating, like the tropical storm advancing on New Amsterdam. On one side nature's wrath on the other, man's. No contest, if you stacked one up against the other, but this time man had a head start.

He would have to keep the weather in mind when he planned his surprise at the airport. Nothing could be lef to chance.

The Executioner hadn't survived this long by being careless in his preparations, nor would he be letting down his guard in this case, when his life was riding on the line

For starters, he would use a different phone booth when he called Encizo, checking out the safe house first. In case

The rental car's engine answered to his first touch of the key and Bolan set off under slate gray skies, rain drumming on the windshield.

It was perfect, how the weather fit his mood.

"YOU'RE LEAVING?"

There was something close to panic in Alicia's voice, but she controlled it in a heartbeat, bearing up.

Encizo studied her for several seconds, then finally said "I have some work to do."

"More killing," she responded. "With your friend, Belasko."

"You have problems in New Amsterdam you haven' even recognized," the Cuban said, sidestepping her challenge for the moment. "Trusting people only works if they're trustworthy."

"You made a promise to my father."

"And I've kept it."

"Until now."

"I have a job to do," Encizo told her, "and it isn't passing out leaflets in shopping malls or listening to speeches in the park. Your father's opposition won't back off until he's ruined, maybe dead. If they can't earn a winning margin on election day, they'll buy one, steal it—anything they have to do."

"The balloting is supervised," Alicia answered, sitting with her back against the headboard, sheets drawn up beneath her chin.

Encizo didn't have much time before the rendezvous with Bolan, but he couldn't leave like this.

"Suppose your father pulls it off," he said. "What then? You think Castillo and his sponsors will evaporate and eat their losses? Guess again. They'll take your father out by any means available—a scandal or a bullet, they don't care—and what comes next? A new election, maybe, to select a suitable replacement?"

"The United Nations—"

"Hasn't even recognized New Amsterdam," he interrupted her. "Suppose they speed up the process in your case, though I wouldn't hold my breath if I were you. Then what? Somebody kills your father and a new election's scheduled, nice and legal. Don't confuse the UN with a bunch of homicide detectives. Even if they were suspicious, it's beyond their jurisdiction, barring some kind of continuing unrest. At most they might decline to recognize Castillo's government. That hurts the overall economy, but wouldn't do a thing to interrupt the traffic in cocaine."

"You paint a hopeless picture."

"Not at all. We still have ways of dealing with Castillo, but they may not lie within the letter of the law."

"You mean to kill him?"

"At the moment I'm more interested in his silent partners. The Colombians and Cubans. They're your major threat. Castillo's just a puppet dancing on their string."

"So you would kill the others."

"If I have to."

"You dismiss their lives so easily," Alicia said.

"As they do yours." Encizo hesitated, frowning. "Look, I really don't have time for a debate. Havana has a team of reinforcements on the way. My friend needs help."

"You'd better go, then." Just like that, dismissing him.

"You're safe here if you don't tell anybody where you are," he said.

"I won't, but I must leave soon."

"Why?"

"My father needs me."

"Something tells me he can get along just fine."

"Then let's say I need him. I need to be involved. I can't sit back and watch, especially if the last few days of the campaign are going to be stained with blood."

Encizo had no choice. "I wish you'd reconsider, but it's still your call."

Her voice reached out and caught him at the door. "Be careful?"

Turning back to face her, Encizo was startled by the tears on her cheeks.

"I always am," he said.

It wasn't strictly true, of course. His work with Phoenix Force involved substantial—some would say outrageous—risks to life and limb. But "careful" was a state of mind, involving strategy and expertise. It wasn't limited to simply steering clear of danger situations. Encizo had always made his living in the trenches, so to speak, and he expected he would die there someday.

But it wouldn't be from carelessness or lack of trying to succeed.

His enemies might overpower him someday, but they would never catch him with his guard down.

IT WAS RAINING when Encizo hit the street. He stayed close to the buildings for what shelter they could offer, watching out for Bolan's car. The pickup point was two blocks north and one block east, but the Executioner would be cruising, checking out the neighborhood—standard procedure in hostile territory.

The Smith & Wesson Model 411 automatic in Encizo's belt gave him a bit more confidence than if he had been walking down the street unarmed. He could defend himself if he was ambushed, but the odds would still be long against him.

As he waited on the corner, he had time to check his watch and see that he was forty seconds early. Glancing up, he saw the dark sedan pull in against the curb, Mack Bolan at the wheel. Encizo got a soaking on the short run to the car, and then he was inside, the door shut tight behind him.

"Ready?" Bolan asked.

"Whenever you are."

"How's the lady?"

"Getting by. She won't stay put, though. Wants to help her father out."

"Her choice," the Executioner replied.

"That's what I told her."

"Fair enough." They were already rolling toward the next main intersection, winding toward the airport. "How's it feel," asked Bolan, "riding in the hospitality wagon?"

Encizo stared out his window, streaked with rain. "Feels good," he said. "I hope they aren't expecting service with a smile."

HERNANDO CRISTOBAL WAS sipping coffee when the seat belt lights came on inside the cabin of the old aircraft. He drained his cup and left it on the tray for the attendant to retrieve when she was ready. Staring out the window, he saw only water below, rain streaked across the Plexiglas, but they were banking now, and he would soon be looking at the green coast of New Amsterdam. As green as it could be, that was, with stormy weather closing in.

It had been seven years since Cristobal's last visit to the island. He wasn't especially looking forward to it now, but this was business. He was under orders, and he couldn't fail.

There were one hundred fifty other passengers on board. His traveling companions sat together, more or less. Miguel Estrada was on his right, the aisle seat, the others filling the two short rows behind them.

Each man had his specialty within the DGI, from sabotage to the gathering of raw intelligence, cryptography, assassination, money laundering. Hernando Cristobal outranked them all, though it wasn't apparent when he wore civilian clothes. He was the smallest of the six in terms of stature, but his military bearing still shone through. The members of his team had had to practice casual behavior in his presence to refrain from the salutes and general show of deference that was his due in Cuba.

The tropical storm didn't concern him overmuch. One didn't come of age in Cuba without living through sporadic hurricanes. The worst that Cristobal remembered, from his early years, had wrecked his family home in Manzanillo. He could still recall his father, standing in the rain-soaked wreckage, muttering dire curses to himself, too proud to cry.

It was a different world these days since the defection of the spineless Soviets to an imitation of the West. Marx and Lenin would be spinning in their graves, if they had been possessed of souls. How swiftly and easily the Russians had given up their principles, abandoning seventy years of sacrifice and devotion to pursue the almighty dollar.

Only Fidel stood fast, and even he was getting on in years. Cristobal knew that there would have to be a new chief in Havana one day soon, and he was working overtime to place himself among the first rank of contenders for the throne. If he could help ensure a triumph in New Amsterdam—the first gain in a decade marked by crushing losses—it could only place him that much closer to his goal.

There had been trouble in Hollandia, though details were obscure. For weeks, Armand Castillo's campaign had been nearly flawless, even with the upstart opposition running hard in second place. But now there was a new threat on the scene, still undefined, although Castillo seemed to think that the Americans were somehow meddling in the race.

Perhaps. Hernando Cristobal would judge that for himself when he had scrutinized the evidence and grilled Castillo privately. Meanwhile his mind was open to a range of possibilities. He didn't trust the Medellín cartel by any means, despite their frank devotion to personal profit regardless of political ideology. It wouldn't be beyond the Colombians to subvert their own cause if they thought it would bring them more cash.

Possibilities.

The answers would be waiting for him on the ground.

They were over land now, leveling off into the approach. The landing gear was locked in place as the four Proteus 765 turboprops powered back. Cristobal kept his eyes fixed on the rain-streaked window, waiting for the solid thump of touchdown on the runway, finally relaxing when it came.

They taxied to the terminal and Cristobal lined up to leave the plane. With his companions, he was traveling as a consultant for a new resort hotel firm, part of Castro's effort to "modernize" Cuba without sacrificing the gains of the holy People's Revolution. Thus far, no hotels had been constructed, but the firm provided decent cover for DGI operatives traveling around the Caribbean and Latin America.

Customs and immigration were no problem, a simple rubber-stamp procedure with perfunctory questions asked and answered. They spent more time waiting for their luggage, and even that was no great inconvenience. Thirty minutes after touchdown, Cristobal and his companions were leaving the terminal, snapping their umbrellas open for the short walk to their waiting rental cars.

Two vehicles, with three men each. A short ride would take them to their luxury hotel downtown, with quarters suited to a group of stylish businessmen. From there, it would be simple to contact Armand Castillo on the telephone and arrange a meeting.

"Down there."

Cristobal recognized the cars from their description at the rental counter and the license numbers printed on the plastic tags that dangled from the keys.

Bent forward under the umbrella, he set off with long strides toward the waiting cars.

THE TIP FROM STONY MAN hadn't included names or physical descriptions of his targets, but the Executioner filled in the blanks himself, with some help from Rafael Encizo and a bit of simple bribery. Encizo posed as a policeman, flashing his credentials to obtain a passenger list for the incoming Cubana Airlines flight, and fifty dollars to a rental clerk had singled out a group of six men traveling alone, with two cars waiting in the pickup lot.

From there, Encizo did the rest, with his encyclopedic knowledge of the DGI. He loitered near the immigration desk and recognized Hernando Cristobal, a colonel in the Cuban secret service, with his flunkies trailing after him like chicks behind a mother hen.

They were waiting in the rain when Cristobal and company emerged, resembling animated mushrooms with their matching black umbrellas, trooping toward the lot that held their rental cars. Encizo watched them through binoculars, while Bolan used the Walther WA-2000's Schmidt & Bender scope.

Six rounds, six targets, at a range of something under eighty yards. It should be easy if he didn't rush it, make the first shot count and follow through with fluid grace, no pausing to assess the hits before he finished off his magazine.

They had considered using plastic charges on the vehicles, but it was cleaner with the rifle, less chance of endangering civilians. As it was, the rain was keeping casual strollers under cover, many new arrivals waiting in the terminal to see if there would be a break before they made the dash to waiting rental cars.

And there was no time like the present.

"Ready."

Bolan spoke as much to himself as to Encizo, lining up the cross hairs on Hernando Cristobal, a head shot through the flimsy screen of the umbrella. He squeezed gently on the Walther's trigger, taking up the slack.

The rifle lurched against his shoulder, the first Winchester Magnum round well on its way as he swung the Walther's muzzle a half inch to the right, making target acquisition on his second mark.

"One down." Encizo confirmed the first kill even as Bolan squeezed the rifle's trigger a second time.

Two away, and he was tracking the third man in line before his targets understood that something was terribly, fatally wrong.

Number Three tried to save himself, dropping his umbrella and turning to run. He lost traction on the rain-slicked pavement, slamming into Number Four, the two of them almost falling, keeping their balance only by clinging to each other.

Bolan squeezed the rifle's trigger twice more, the two shots ripping out almost as one, his targets mashing together in a cheek-to-cheek embrace. Bright crimson splashed in the Schmidt & Bender sight as Bolan swung on to another target, tracking.

Number Five was running for his life, incongruously clinging to his umbrella, elbows pumping as he ran, the black dome bobbing up and down above his head. Bolan drew a bead between his shoulder blades and fired again, the Walther's fifth round sizzling downrange.

The explosive impact punched the Cuban forward, airborne, covering the space of three long strides without his wing tips ever touching solid ground. He went down on his face and slithered on the pavement, arms outflung to either side, the black umbrella finally slipping from his fingers, wobbling out of reach.

And that left one.

Sheer force of habit had the sole survivor reaching for a pistol he had left behind in Cuba. Even as he realized the error, Number Six was turning on his heel, prepared to dodge behind the nearest rental car to try to save himself that way.

It almost worked.

One foot was off the pavement in a classic runner's stance, a statue poised and ready, straining forward, when the last of Bolan's rounds slammed into his chest. The Cuban stumbled sideways, lost his balance and wound up on one knee. He clapped a hand across the bloody geyser spouting from his rib cage, trying to stop the flow, but there was nothing he could do. His mangled lungs gave up an instant later, and he toppled slowly forward on his face.

Six up, six down.

The warrior took another moment to survey the carnage. One man lay twitching feebly, but he wouldn't last for long. The pool of blood beneath him was spreading, rapidly diluted, sluiced away by driving rain.

"Let's go."

He stood the Walther in its toolbox, closed the lid and latched it. Encizo slid behind the wheel of their vehicle and they got out of there, rain drumming on the windshield. The weather would increase their lag time with security and the police. Bolan had no fear of their being intercepted as they left the airport and headed back toward town.

The Cuban delegation had been intercepted. It would send a shock wave all the way back to Havana, but the local game was still in progress, going strong.

Castillo would be shaken by the latest strike...or would he be relieved? Removal of the Cuban overseers would let him play the game his way, as much as that was possible with Medellín involved.

Whatever happened, Bolan meant to be on top of it, prepared to take advantage of the opposition's weak points as they were revealed, a war of attrition, grinding down the enemy until he lost his will and his ability to fight.

It struck him suddenly how they could take advantage of the DGI's fiasco at the airport, now, before the shock waves from the shooting spread throughout Hollandia.

A little extra something for the enemy.

A special twist, to leave him swinging in the wind.

9

Armand Castillo took his whiskey straight. On days like this, he went for double shots to calm his nerves. At present he was working on his fourth drink of the evening, and it hadn't done the job.

A TV bulletin had briefed him on the shooting at the airport, just enough to set his teeth on edge before he checked it out and learned the details for himself. Before he started making calls, Castillo knew it was the Cuban delegation, dead and gone before he even had a chance to speak to them.

But how?

The airport shooting, to Castillo's mind, was the most frightening event so far, since things had started getting out of hand. He reckoned anyone could spot the Obregons if they were looking hard enough, but the arrival of the DGI "consultants" had been strictly secret, plotted in Havana and relayed to him directly via telephone, his private line. It was beyond Castillo, how his enemies—whoever they might be—had managed to discover when the Cubans were arriving, who they represented, which specific passengers from the Cubana Airlines flight were on the team.

Another double, more or less, and he would have to break the bad news to his handler in Havana. It wouldn't be pleasant, and he knew the bulletin would only make him seem incompetent, despite the fact that it was obviously not his fault. If there were leaks involved, they would be on the other end, in Cuba, but convincing his control of that would be impossible.

The sudden shrilling of the telephone, his private line again, surprised Castillo, almost made him spill the remnants of his drink. He saved it, though, and threw the whiskey back before he lifted the receiver midway through the second ring.

"Hello?"

"I was surprised by the reception at the airport," said a stranger's Cuban-accented voice.

Castillo hesitated, fumbling for an answer, settling for, "Excuse me, but there must be some—"

"Mistake?" the caller interrupted. "If there is, Armand, I think it must be yours."

"Who is this?"

"A survivor."

"But—"

"The six were not advised of my assignment," the caller said. "It was felt that they—and you—should be evaluated independently. In the event of any problems, I was given ultimate authority."

Castillo sat down in the nearest chair. It felt as if a ton of weight had settled on his shoulders, bearing him down.

"What is it that you want?" he asked.

"A meeting. There is danger close to you, beyond what you have recognized so far."

Castillo felt the short hairs rising on his nape. "What do you mean?"

"Not on the telephone."

Almost before Castillo had a chance to understand what he was hearing, the stranger had specified a time and place for their meeting, a suburban park, the northeast quarter of Hollandia.

"And come alone."

"My driver—"

"No one may be trusted at the moment, do you understand?"

In fact, Castillo didn't understand at all, but he wasn't about to say so and thus make himself appear more foolish than he did already. It was bad enough, the violence

that Castillo and his friends had suffered, but now hi
Cuban sponsors were involved, as well.

Where would it end?

"You'll be there?"

"Yes." Castillo had no choice. If he refused, the DG
might very well retaliate against him physically, withou
another warning. He had seen their work before, first
hand, and didn't relish stepping through his door som
morning to receive a bullet in the head.

The link was broken and he cradled the receiver, cut
ting off the loud, insistent dial tone. He could hear th
wind and rain outside, no thunder yet, but it would be
miserable night for meeting someone in the park.

No doubt his contact would be counting on the weathe
for protection, after the fiasco at the airport. It was dar
out now, and if Castillo wasn't followed, they should hav
a decent chance of meeting unobserved.

Again he felt a pang of fear. Suppose it was a trap? As
sassins might be waiting for him at the rendezvous, thei
only message issuing from pistols.

The caller had referred to danger close at hand, pre
sumably within his own campaign staff, closer than Cas
tillo recognized.

All right then, he was hooked. He had to learn the an
swer to that riddle, or he knew that it would haunt him
drive him to distraction.

Danger. There was certainly enough of that to go aroun
these days.

Castillo was a born survivor, and he meant to save him
self at any cost. Whatever else transpired, he meant t
come out on the other side alive.

It was never too late to start watching your back.

Castillo took a pistol from his desk and stuck it in th
waistband of his slacks before he fetched his raincoat an
umbrella and headed for the night outside.

ENCIZO HAD PLACED his call to Castillo from a phon
booth near the park to give himself some lead time at th
rendezvous. Bolan's plan was good, persuading Castill

that an unexpected member of the DGI inspection team had managed to survive the airport ambush. There would be no way to verify his presence in New Amsterdam short of calling Havana, and Encizo didn't think Castillo was about to take that step.

Not with the problems he already had on tap.

The rain had faded for a time, but it was back in force now, drumming on Encizo's head and shoulders as he left the phone booth and moved toward his compact rental car. He put the vehicle in motion, turned left on the narrow road that cut the park in two and drove until he reached the ornate bandstand about one hundred yards from where he had started. There, he parked and killed the engine, switching off the headlights and waiting in the rainy darkness for his contact to arrive.

There was a chance Castillo might ignore his orders, but the Phoenix Force warrior didn't think it likely. He had recognized the fear and indecision in Castillo's voice while they were talking on the telephone. He had the mole's attention with his warning of potential danger close at hand—enough to bring Castillo out, at any rate, to learn who might be plotting his destruction.

After waiting twenty minutes in the rain, Encizo saw headlights probing through the darkness, glinting off the streaks of water plunging from a saturated sky. There would be lightning soon as the tropical storm approached, gaining force and velocity until it earned the label of a hurricane.

But not just yet.

Encizo flashed his headlights when the new arrival had approached within a range of twenty yards. This was the risky time, when hidden guns might open fire and riddle him before he had a chance to flee. It was a gamble, more or less, and he was betting on Castillo's curiosity, his talent for self-preservation.

The mole couldn't afford to double-cross a possible connection with the DGI, especially if the stranger had specific information that would save Castillo's reputation...or his life. A trick at this point could rebound against Castillo in disastrous terms. He would not give the order for a homicide until he knew whom he was killing, what he stood to gain or lose by snuffing out that certain life.

The cars were almost nose to nose before Castillo killed his lights and engine, racing through the downpour to slide in beside Encizo, dripping in the shotgun seat. Castillo squinted in the darkness, making an attempt to recognize this stranger from his days around Havana, any clue at all, and getting nowhere fast.

Encizo bypassed the amenities and went directly to the point. "Six valued officers," he said. "They won't be easy to replace."

"I understand."

"Who else, beside yourself, knew they were coming?"

Castillo didn't even have to think about it. "No one but Gutierrez."

"Ah." The name meant zilch to Encizo, but it would fit some kind of go-between who handled details with the Cubans for Castillo. "Was he at the airport?"

"No," Castillo said. "The orders were to wait until the team made contact, follow their instructions for the meeting."

"I'm aware of the instructions," Encizo said, lying through his teeth. "I'm trying to find out if they were followed."

"I gave no contrary orders to Ramon."

Ramon Gutierrez. They were making progress.

"There is something you must know about Ramon," Encizo said. "We have discovered indications that his loyalty may be . . . flexible."

Castillo blinked, lurched backward in his seat as if Encizo had just offered him a plate of worms and grubs to eat. "It cannot be! He was selected, handpicked by—"

"I know," Encizo interrupted. "Much has come to light within the past few hours. We believe now that he might have been recruited by another party."

There it was, the kiss of death. He read it in Castillo's face. The man was furious, already plotting vengeance on his aide-de-camp.

"I will take care of it," Castillo said.

"Not yet. We wish to verify his treason first, through observation."

"Is that necessary?"

"We would not demand it otherwise!"

"Of course." The candidate was chastened. "I was only thinking of the risk he poses to our effort."

"There will be no risk," Encizo said, "if you maintain surveillance. Keep him busy with peripheral concerns and watch him closely. When his contact is revealed, then we can strike."

"You think he is in league with the Americans?"

It was the logical assumption from Castillo's point of view. Encizo almost smiled before he punctured that balloon.

"In fact," he said, "we think he might be working against your friends from Medellín."

Castillo blanched at that, his shoulders slumping.

"No!"

"We could be wrong, of course."

"What can we do?"

"If you would save yourself, then you must follow my instructions to the letter. First . . ."

THE SAFE HOUSE HAD BEGUN to feel more like a prison cell. Alicia Grandier had spent the hour since Raul Camacho left her grappling with mixed emotions: fear and anger; unexpected passion; guilt at having gone to bed with Raul, and yet again for hiding like a coward when her father needed her.

Of course, he wouldn't say so. Quite the opposite, in fact. When she had called him, careful not to say where she was staying, he had urged her to forget about the campaign and protect herself. Alicia knew from the inflection of his voice that he was worried, even frightened. And that knowledge, more than anything else, had amplified her own internal fears.

Thinking back to childhood, she could visualize her father in a wide variety of moods and situations. She had seen him happy, celebrating some achievement, even slightly drunk on two or three occasions. At the other extreme, she had seen him angry to the point of rage, and racked with grief on the occasion of her mother's death.

But she had never seen him scared before.

Regardless of the threats that he received, the various attacks against the paper or himself, Alicia couldn't think of one occasion when her father had been less than confident and self-assured. If he was frightened now, it meant that things were worse than ever in the past, the risks at once more urgent and extreme.

Alicia knew that she was part of it. The several attacks aimed at her would do more to worry her father than any threat directed at him or the rest of his staff. She was all he had left in terms of family, and so she understood his urging her to hide until the danger was past. It was a parent's natural reaction, but she couldn't bring herself to follow his instructions.

She was leaving, going back to work on the campaign. Her father needed her now more than ever, and she wouldn't desert him in the crunch. They had an election to win, and Alicia would be standing at his side when they reached the finish line, come what may.

It felt strange leaving, even so. Within the past few hours, the apartment had become her sanctuary and her unexpected love nest. She was still not certain what had moved her to share such intimacy with a virtual stranger. True, he had saved her life repeatedly in the space of one day, forging a unique bond of trust, but there was more to it than that. She was attracted to this man of violence in a way she didn't fully understand...and that, too, frightened her, compelling her to get away, regain the trappings of her normal life at any cost.

When she had toweled off from the shower, finished dressing in her rumpled clothes, Alicia wandered through the small apartment, making sure that she left nothing of her own behind. Raul knew where to find her if he cared enough to look, but she couldn't sit there and let her father face the enemy alone.

She had no car, but there was money in her purse, and taxis were available. She made the call on Raul's phone, remembering at the last moment not to have the taxi stop outside of the apartment house. Instead she named the nearest major intersection, gave herself five minutes for the walk and cradled the receiver, satisfied that she had done her best to keep Camacho's hideaway secure.

He hadn't left her with a key to lock the dead bolt, but she managed to secure the other lock behind her as she left. There was no turning back from that point on. The residential street was dark and quiet, no one visible from where she stood. The rain had slackened off for the present, but the wind was picking up. It took a moment for Alicia to regain her nerve and put her feet in motion, pacing off the sidewalk to the corner, turning north to walk another block to meet her cab.

She wasn't being paranoid at that point, she decided, as she listened for the sound of footsteps coming up behind her, watched for shadow figures loitering in vehicles against the curb. Three attacks in one day, at least two of them meant to be lethal, convinced her that she was correct in watching her back. At this point she would be a fool if she didn't believe in someone laying plans to harm her.

Still, she didn't take it personally, in the sense of someone who had been harassed by private enemies. Her father was the primary target, his enemies prepared to stop at nothing in their effort to demolish his campaign. Alicia was a pawn, a handle toward that end, and knowing that diminished her fear slightly, allowing the warm flush of anger to return.

Castillo and his cronies thought so little of her that they felt she would submit to their destructive game. Raul and Mike Belasko had prevented them from grabbing her so far, but now Alicia felt a need to stand up for herself. She might not be a fighter, schooled in weaponry or martial arts, but she could hurt her father's enemies in other ways—by standing fast and coming back to work for his campaign despite her private fears, ensuring that his enemies didn't succeed in scaring her away and thereby hampering the campaign effort in its final days.

It was little enough, but all she could do at the moment.

The real fighting, Alicia understood, was best left to others.

She reached the corner, crossed the street and walked north through shadows pooled between the widely separated streetlights, sidewalk slick and wet beneath her feet. When a car passed halfway down the block, she didn't hesitate or break her stride. Exuding confidence and self-control, in spite of how she really felt, Alicia reached the intersection, waiting in the doorway of a small hotel until the taxi arrived.

The driver saw her coming and waited for her to take her seat in the back. She gave him the address of her father's campaign headquarters, preferring to stop by the office and work for a while on her own rather than head directly back to the house. It would help her, she thought, to sit at her desk and perform normal tasks for an hour or so before she confronted her father again and resumed the argument about her safety.

She was an adult now.

She would do as she saw fit, and not as she was told.

ARMAND CASTILLO GULPED his whiskey and tried to put his jumbled thoughts in order. It was difficult to cope with all that he had learned this evening, making sense of what appeared to be a wicked joke.

But there could be no doubt about it. His DGI contact from Havana hadn't been laughing when he dropped the bomb about Ramon Gutierrez.

Traitor.

In his wildest dreams, Castillo never would have guessed. Gutierrez had been sent to him directly from

Cuba, with the reputation of a man who got things done at any cost. Thus far, if anyone had asked Castillo, he would readily have said Gutierrez was performing as required. There seemed to be no problem, up until the past few hours, when Ramon and his selected thugs began to drop the ball.

It was suspicious, certainly, this sudden lapse—four of Ramon's men beaten, one of them hospitalized in intensive care, and three others killed in the course of two confrontations with the same solitary man. It made no sense, even in conjunction with the spate of violence directed at the Obregons...unless, perhaps, Gutierrez was deliberately failing in his duties now, when he was needed most.

The plot, as outlined to Castillo, was simplicity itself. According to his DGI control, Ramon had gone in business for himself, with a competitor from Bogotá whose cash reserve and private army rivaled the resources of the Medellín cartel. Gutierrez was allegedly prepared to sell out Castillo, betray the Obregons, his masters in Havana—all to make himself a wealthy man. An unnamed candidate was being groomed to lead a new campaign if neither Grandier nor Castillo survived the present race with sufficient votes to win a clear majority.

Or, more to the point, if neither survived it at all.

The prospect of defeat was one thing, but the threat of death had never crossed Castillo's mind until he heard the thought expressed in no uncertain terms. It could be done in any one of several ways—to cast the blame on Martin Grandier, perhaps, or simply leave a mystery behind. Another possible scenario would blame the Obregons, insinuate a falling out, and thus destroy Castillo's reputation even as his flesh was laid to rest.

Blind fury vied with panic, and Castillo poured himself another double shot of whiskey. He was feeling the effects of several drinks already, but he needed more. His mind was racing, and he hoped the alcohol would slow it a bit, allow him to collect his thoughts, assess his options.

The first impulse, on learning of Ramon's betrayal, had been to retaliate with crushing force. Castillo would have gladly done the job himself, but he had been dissuaded by the agent from Havana. It was better to observe Ramon, the stranger said, and counter any moves he made as they occurred. In that way, Gutierrez could be managed and controlled, potential damage minimized.

It ran against the grain, this waiting for a traitor to make his next move. If the DGI was so sure of Ramon's betrayal, why should he live another day? It seemed unnecessarily risky to Castillo, but he reminded himself that he wasn't in command. He was merely following orders, playing his part in a game that was suddenly more complicated and dangerous than he had imagined. He would have bailed out, given half a chance, but Havana would never stand for that, and neither would the Obregons.

Thinking of the brothers from Medellín, Castillo felt a sudden chill. Suppose they learned of Ramon's duplicity and somehow imagined that Castillo was responsible, a part of the conspiracy against them? There would be no hesitation from Francisco when it came to settling that kind of score. Castillo would be lucky if he got off with a bullet in the head and there would be no warning.

He set the empty glass on his desk and opened the lower right-hand drawer, rummaging beneath some papers for the pistol he kept hidden there. It was a 9 mm Llama M-82, and while he rarely carried the weapon, Castillo was proficient in its use. In practice on the firing range, he could deliver sixteen rounds on target any time he wanted to.

And now he wondered if it would feel any different, firing at a man.

Of course, he had armed bodyguards to deal with that contingency, but most of them had been retained by Gutierrez and all were now suspect. It terrified Castillo to think that the very men he depended on to protect him might be enemies, but there was nothing he could do about it at the moment. Any wholesale turnover in staff would alert Gutierrez, and a plea for bodyguards from the Obregon brothers would tell them that something was drastically wrong.

Above all Castillo knew he had to preserve appearances, at least until the DGI informed him it was time to deal with Ramon's treachery in some permanent fashion.

The candidate found himself looking forward to that day with great anticipation. He would ask to execute the traitor himself, insist if possible.

It was only fair. Simple justice demanded nothing less.

10

There was more to the Flame Club, in downtown Hollandia, than met the eye. Out front, it was a stylish supper club with seating for five hundred guests, live music and dancing after 9:00 p.m. In back, accessible by invitation only, was a lavish gambling casino in the best Las Vegas style, catering to high rollers with a taste for hot and heavy action. Gambling was illegal in New Amsterdam, but local cops were paid to let it slide. Since it was only gambling for wealthy tourists, nothing dirty, they were happy to oblige.

The owner of the Flame Club was Francisco Obregon.

It was unlikely, in Mack Bolan's view, that the authorities knew much—or anything—about the nightclub's other function. Obregon maintained an office on the second floor, above the gaming room, which doubled as a field command post and a private bank. His business dealt exclusively in cash, regardless of the day or hour, and Francisco couldn't always wait for banking hours to close a deal. He kept a hefty sum at home, of course, but for those special moments, when he needed cash in seven figures at the crack of dawn or noon on Christmas Day, the office at the Flame Club served his needs.

It was about to serve the Executioner, as well.

Bad weather hadn't kept the party animals away as far as Bolan could determine. He ignored the club's valet and parked his rental on the south side of the building, close enough to reach in a hurry if he had to. He had changed into a dinner jacket for the outing, cut to hide the 93-R in its shoulder rig, and no one gave him a second glance as he entered the club.

The maître d' examined Bolan briefly, putting on a smile before the Executioner brushed past him, circled the dining room and moved on in the direction of the narrow hall that led to the casino tucked away behind the scenes. Instead of going that route though, he took the stairs, unbuttoning his jacket as he reached the landing on the second floor.

The guard was young, midtwenties, but he had a killer's eyes. He didn't flinch from Bolan even when the Executioner was in his face. The young man knew a gringo when he saw one, and he spoke English with an accent that was strictly Medellín.

"You lookin' for the toilet, man, is not up here."

"I'm looking for the manager," Bolan replied, putting on an easy smile. "You want to tell him or shall I?"

"He's busy. You got an appointment?"

"Special invitation," Bolan answered as his right hand slipped inside the dinner jacket, finding the Beretta.

Instantly the young man made a grab to reach his own piece, almost making it. He might have beaten his opponent to the draw, but he wasn't prepared for Bolan's left hand, slashing forward with the fingers rigid, clenched into a blade of flesh and bone. His larynx took the brunt of Bolan's jab, not lethal, but enough to take his mind off guns and leave him retching on his knees.

When he recovered, he was staring down the maw of the Executioner's side arm, watching as his own gun found a place in Bolan's belt. The youngster offered no resistance as a strong hand brought him to his feet and spun him toward the office door.

"No tricks," Bolan warned. "Play it straight, and you just might see the sun come up tomorrow."

Without a word the young man raised a fist and rapped twice on the door, hesitated a heartbeat, then rapped once more. A latch was thrown inside, and Bolan shoved the sentry forward as the door began to open, following immediately on his heels.

A beefy older man waiting just across the threshold was jolted backward by the impact of the door and Bolan's escort. He was groping beneath his jacket for a pistol when the 93-R coughed once and a silenced parabellum round drilled through his forehead and slammed him over backward on the carpet in a lifeless sprawl.

The manager was on his feet behind a spacious desk, hands empty, stretched out at his sides as if to demonstrate that he wasn't a threat. Bolan shoved the outside man in that direction, watched him stumble on the corpse and catch himself before he sprawled facedown across the desk. The young man glowered as he got his balance back and made his way around the desk to stand beside the office manager, while Bolan kicked the door shut with his heel.

"I'll keep it simple," he informed the chunky forty-something manager. "I want what's in the safe. You've got the combination. I'd prefer to leave you breathing, but it's your call either way."

"Who are you?"

"Let's say that I've been following Francisco's progress on the island. He's about to have a major problem. This is part of it."

"You don't know what you're doing," the manager said.

"If I was looking for an argument, I'd take a shot at politics," Bolan replied. "Now, unless you want to join your friend, here—" he nodded toward the body on the floor "—I would suggest you fill that briefcase and make it quick."

The manager had used up all the breath he had to spare for small talk. Bolan tracked him with his pistol as he came around the desk and headed for the large safe in the corner. Bending low, he spun the dial this way and that, four digits, finally opening the door on stacks of currency including guilders, large-denomination notes for Colombian peace and American greenbacks.

"Start with the American," Bolan instructed, watching closely as the manager emptied his leather briefcase and

egan to fill it with banded stacks of hundred-dollar bills.
e estimated that the bag held nearly a quarter-million
ollars when the manager ran out of room and dropped
e lid, securing the latches with his thumbs.

"You have another bag?" Bolan asked.

Slowly, grudgingly, the night man nodded.

"Don't look so glum," Bolan said. "Guilders this time.
arge denominations. If it helps, just tell yourself it's go-
ng to a worthy cause."

It didn't help, if the expression on the manager's round
ace was any indication. Still, he did as he was told, and
olan watched him close the second case, a leather satchel
ot unlike a doctor's bag.

"That's fine," he said, and pumped a parabellum round
nto the telephone that occupied a corner of the roomy
esk. The manager recoiled in fear, the younger man re-
aining where he was, a dark scowl on his face.

"No point in taking chances," Bolan stated as he re-
ieved the bags, tucked one beneath his left arm, while the
ther filled his hand. "If you've got half the brains I give
ou credit for, you'll wait awhile before you hit the panic
utton."

He was turning toward the door and freedom when the
oung man made his move, a dive in the direction of the
rostrate corpse, hands reaching for the dead man's pis-
ol.

Too damned macho for his own good.

Bolan swung around and shot him twice before the
unner reached his destination, parabellum shockers rip-
ing through the crown of his skull, leaving him draped
cross the other body at an angle.

"Bad choice," he told the manager, and closed the door
ehind him, moving swiftly toward the stairs. His gun was
ut of sight before he reached the dining room, retreating
ast the puzzled maître d'.

Outside, it had begun to rain again and heavily, but Bo-
an hardly noticed. He was smiling as he reached the rental
ar and slid behind the wheel.

It wasn't often that he turned a profit on his private war, but there were times when fortune gave him a nod. Like now. The Obregons were just about to fund their own defeat.

THE OPEN DEAD BOLT TOLD Encizo that Alicia had departed from the safehouse. He wasn't especially surprised, considering her independence and the store she set by helping in her father's race for office. There was nothing he could do in realistic terms to save the lady from herself. If she was bent on taking chances, then so be it.

Still, it worried him, and he took time to sort the feelings out as he prowled through the empty rooms.

A part of it was duty, to be sure. He was assigned to work with the campaign when not assisting Bolan on the street, protect Alicia and her father to the best of his ability. So far, the job had been divided, most of Encizo's attention focusing on the woman by a quirk of circumstance. Her father had a team of bodyguards around him while Alicia went off on her own or with a few young volunteers to scout the town for votes.

But there was more to it than that, the Cuban warrior grudgingly admitted to himself. He had begun to care about this woman in a manner that was unprofessional—at best a troublesome distraction; and at worst a fatal error.

She could get him killed without half trying, if he let his mind begin to wander from the reason for his visit to New Amsterdam. It was about the DGI and drugs from Medellín infesting paradise, corrupting everything they touched, converting the pursuit of independence into something dark and sinister.

There was no place for romance on the battlefield, and now he wondered if the passion that had flared between Alicia and himself had driven her to flee the safehouse looking for another place to hide.

Where would she go if she was running?

Encizo considered it for several moments, finally shaking his head. The woman wouldn't run away, he told himself. Retreat wasn't her style. The attacks she had survived that day would frighten her, of course, but she wouldn't allow that fear to slow her down. If anything, she would demand more of herself as a result of what her enemies had done, a show of inner strength to hurl the threat back in their faces.

That meant trouble, and he turned his mind to thinking where she might have gone if she was going to resume her work. Her father's house, perhaps. It would be worth a look, in case she headed there to reassure him she was safe.

Encizo checked the answering machine, but there had been no messages since Bolan's call before their foray to the airport. As for outgoing calls, he had no way of knowing if Alicia had used the telephone or not. She had no car on hand, which meant that she was either walking or she had made arrangements for a ride. In that event...

He stopped himself before the train of thought could take him any further. He didn't believe she would have compromised the safehouse, but if so, the damage was already done. The best that he could do was take himself away from there without delay and try to find out where Alicia was.

He lifted the telephone receiver and tapped out Martin Grandier's home number from memory. A man's voice answered, cautious, permitting a note of relief as "Raul Camacho" identified himself. The relief disappeared abruptly when he asked for Alicia, the houseman asking when he and the lady had been separated.

So much for the home front.

Encizo kept it vague and disengaged as rapidly as possible. He tried Alicia's own apartment next, and let the phone ring half a dozen times before he gave it up.

That narrowed down the field. In fact, the only other place that came to mind was campaign headquarters. If she had found herself another hideaway—a friend's place or a motel room, for instance—he would never track her down.

At least the office was a possibility, and failing there, he would leave a message for Bolan on the cutout number before he regrouped at Grandier's home in the suburbs.

Encizo double locked the door behind him, then jogged to his car. The nagging sense of urgency was back, a whiff of danger in the air.

As if in answer to his thoughts, a flash of lightning scrawled its mark across the sky, pursued by thunder that reminded him of distant cannon fire.

The calm before the storm was history.

DESPITE THE RAIN, Alicia left her cab a block from party headquarters, preferring to walk for security's sake. If she was being paranoid, the worst that she would suffer was a soaking, possibly a runny nose. But on the other hand, if she was right...

Suppose her father's enemies were staking out the office. What was she supposed to do about it? Slip away and call for help, presumably, but who was there that she could really trust? Her father's aides and bodyguards were simple men, no more than two or three among them with the kind of background that would make them useful in a deadly fight. She knew that some of them were armed these days, against her father's wishes, but there was a world of difference between carrying weapons and using them against another human being.

It occurred to her too late that she had made a serious mistake, not writing down the number of the safehouse where Raul Camacho kept an answering machine. She might not reach him soon enough to be of any help, but he was still her best hope of relief where danger was concerned. Hollandia's police had proved worse than useless during recent weeks, arriving late and taking statements when an incident occurred, apparently unable to discover suspects even with the help of witnesses and photographs.

She thought of Mike Belasko, wondering where he had taken Camacho that night, instantly dismissing the question as one she preferred not to answer. Some riddles were ike that, opening a dark Pandora's box of nightmares. Sometimes it was simply better not to know.

Alicia was a half block from the office, ducking in and out of doorways in an effort to avoid the driving rain, when she caught sight of someone stepping from the building. Even in the rainy darkness, she recognized Erno Soto, his slumped shoulders and forward-jutting head a giveaway to anyone who knew him. He was glancing up and down the street in both directions, stepping off the curb and moving toward a dark sedan that sat directly opposite against the curb. There was a man behind the wheel, but Alicia couldn't see his face.

Not yet.

She stood and watched, cool water streaming down her face, as Soto bent beneath the dome of his umbrella, speaking to the driver of the car. Their conversation wasn't long, and Erno was retreating toward the office when a flash of lightning split the heavens, granting her a brief glimpse of the driver's face—Ramon Gutierrez.

There was no mistake. Alicia knew him well enough before that afternoon's encounter at the shopping mall, Castillo's bullyboy, responsible for most—if not all—of the illegal harassment Alicia's father had suffered throughout the campaign. Whenever there was vandalism, an assault or whispered death threats on the telephone, she knew Ramon Gutierrez was at work.

What was his business here with Erno Soto?

There could only be one answer when she thought it through. The sniveling weasel, Soto, had betrayed her father, sold him out for money or the promise of a power job in government if Castillo became the prime minister. She felt a sudden rush of anger and was about to burst in on the traitor, fire him on the spot . . . when it occurred to her that she should watch and wait a moment, prior to making any hasty moves.

There might be more to learn if she was patient, kept her rage in check and watched her quarry from a cautious distance.

She forgot about the rain, unmindful of the soaking as she stood and waited in the shadows. Thirteen minutes after he went back inside the campaign office, Erno Soto showed himself again. He took time to lock the door, then climbed into his small car waiting out in front. Alicia watched him drive away and counted to ten once he was gone before she took the key ring from her purse and walked toward the office.

Now, to see if she could find out what he had been doing for Gutierrez while pretending that he served her father's cause. For all she knew, there might be evidence in Soto's office, something to support her own eyewitness testimony of his perfidy.

Alicia felt new purpose as she turned the key and let herself inside.

THE PHONE CALL STARTED with a whim, and once the notion put down roots in Bolan's mind, he couldn't let it go. He found a service station that had closed for the night and pulled up beside the phone booth, raindrops spattering his head and shoulders as he made the shift from car to glassed-in cubicle. He fed the box some coins and dialed one of the several numbers he had memorized.

A male voice answered, gruff, suspicious. *"Sí?"*

In English, Bolan asked to speak with Pablo Obregon. The soldier on the other end played dumb, a stall, until Bolan asked him if he thought his boss's life was worth five minutes on the phone. He thought about that for a moment, went away, and Bolan waited for a new voice on the line.

"Who's this?" There was more confidence from this one, with an undertone of irritation shining through.

"Depends on who I'm talking to," the Executioner replied.

"You asked for me, I'm here," Pablo Obregon said.

"Thing is, I'm really looking for your brother."

"Lots of people doing that. I mostly tell them they can go and fuck themselves."

"That's rude."

"I'm hanging up."

"Before I tell you how I spent Francisco's money?" Bolan asked.

He had the dealer's full attention now. "What money?"

"From the Flame Club," Bolan said. "I thought you would have heard about it."

"Listen, man—"

"At a rough count," Bolan said, interrupting him, "I'd say there was about two hundred twenty thousand, just in C-notes. Guilders, say three hundred thousand, give or take."

"You been a very foolish man, my friend."

The warrior smiled and said, "You haven't heard the best part yet. The guilders go to Martin Grandier's campaign. A little something for the war chest, you might say. I think I'll spend the rest of it myself, see how much trouble I can cause Francisco with a quarter-million bucks."

"This is the worst mistake you ever made. The last mistake."

"I guess we'll see," Bolan said. "While we're on the subject, how'd you like the job I did, redecorating your office?"

Pablo thought about that for a moment, letting it sink in before he found his voice. "You're dead, bastard. How's it feel to be a walking dead man?"

"At the moment," Bolan told him, "I feel lucky. Can you still remember how that feels?"

"Enjoy it while you can. You're running out of time."

"I let you slide this morning," Bolan said. "Don't count on any favors next time."

"I can take care of myself."

"I hope so, Pablo. You're about to be an only child."

The dealer sputtered in his rage. "My brother's not afraid of you! You think you're scaring anybody with your little games?"

"I think I scared those fellows in your office pretty good," Bolan said. "Now, I didn't get a chance to check your trousers when the smoke cleared, but I'm guessing that you weren't exactly high and dry."

A torrent of profanity poured through the telephone, Bolan holding the handset away from his ear and waiting for the dealer to regain a vestige of composure. When the curses petered out, he spoke again.

"You need to watch that temper, Pablo. I don't want you dying from a stroke before I have a chance to do the job myself."

"I'll see you dead, you bastard! No one talks to me that way and lives!"

"First time for everything. Think about it while your slacks are at the laundry."

"Mother—"

"When you see Francisco, tell him I'll be coming for him soon. If he's got any personal affairs to put in order, now's the time."

"You think he's scared of you? You think *I'm* scared?"

"I've seen you, Pablo. Don't forget it. Maybe you impress your *pistoleros* with the big talk, but you don't fool me. Next time you're down on all fours, crawling like an animal, you don't get up."

He cradled the receiver, cutting off a stream of curses from the other end. Anger was a weapon to be wielded with discretion. It could add momentum to a killing thrust, or it could tear your enemy apart if he began to act on emotion rather than determined strategy.

The Obregons were sweating. He could smell it from a mile away.

Between the fear and anger, they would soon begin to make mistakes. Perhaps, he thought, they had already started.

It would soon be time to test his theory.

In the meantime though, the Executioner had other business to transact.

11

Armand Castillo had misgivings when he scheduled the private meeting with Gutierrez, but he also knew that he should test himself. They had the best part of two weeks together yet, and if he planned on keeping up a front of confidence and trust, he had to start rehearsing right away.

The challenge would be swallowing his anger, restraining the urge to lean across his desk and seize Gutierrez by the throat. Of course, Castillo realized that he would be no match for the Cuban in hand-to-hand combat. Gutierrez was stronger, in better condition, accustomed to inflicting pain with his bare hands and a variety of tools.

That still left bullets, though. Castillo wore the Llama automatic in his waistband, pressing hard against his lower spine. It would be simple, leaning forward in his chair and smiling at Gutierrez, elbows on the desk, pretending that he had an itch. He could draw and level the pistol at Ramon before the Cuban could react and reach a weapon of his own.

It would be messy, granted, splattering his brains around the study, but Castillo's bodyguards would handle any cleanup chores, no questions asked. Gutierrez would be gone without a trace. If anybody asked, Castillo would present a bland facade of ignorance. The man had simply disappeared, no warning. Who could understand a foreigner? Perhaps, if those who sought him wished to make inquiries in Havana...

Frowning to himself, Castillo watched the fantasy dissolve. He would have loved to kill Gutierrez, but his latest orders were to play along, pretend Ramon was still a trusted confidante and keep him occupied with busywork that wouldn't jeopardize the overall campaign. He would be taken care of when the time was right, by former colleagues of the DGI.

Castillo would have loved to witness that, but there was no way he would be allowed to watch Ramon's undoing. As it was, the candidate felt lucky that Havana didn't view him as a coconspirator. If they suspected him of plotting with Gutierrez to betray the People's Revolution, he would have no hope at all.

This way, at least, he was still in the race, still leading Grandier by two or three percentage points in the most recent poll. He had a fighting chance, and once he was installed as the prime minister, it would become a brand-new game. Havana would think twice about dictating to a head of state, when he could always call on the United States to help him in a crisis. The Obregons would understand, since they disdained the creed of communism anyway. Castillo knew from studying global politics that there were ways to reap financial aid from the United States without surrendering autonomy. He could have millions for defense and still do business with the Obregons. Bolivia, Colombia, Peru and other countries ranging from Mexico to Turkey had been flouting American wishes for years, still rolling in the avalanche of cash.

A dream come true.

The houseman knocked, announced Gutierrez, and Castillo rose to greet the traitor, putting on his politician's smile. They shook hands warmly and Ramon sat down directly opposite the desk, hands folded in his lap. Castillo had been practicing his speech, rehearsing attitudes, deciding on a combination of concern and sympathy.

"What's the progress with the enemy, Ramon?"

Gutierrez shrugged, the corners of his mouth tugged downward in a frown. "The pig who killed my men hasn't been found," he grudgingly admitted. "We're searching for him everywhere. It won't be long."

"I'm thinking it was a mistake to move against Alicia Grandier," Castillo said.

"The brothers started that," Ramon reminded him. "I wasn't trying to abduct her at the mall."

"And what about the park, Ramon?"

"We had to pay the bastard back," Gutierrez answered, stubborn now. "Embarrassment demands reprisal."

"Very well." Castillo thought his tone was perfect, calm and quiet. "But the more you try to punish him, the worse it gets. You still don't know his name?"

"We do," Gutierrez said. "He calls himself Raul Camacho."

"Calls himself?"

"We still have eyes and ears in Grandier's campaign," Gutierrez said. "I'm told the man appeared this morning out of nowhere. Why they took him on, I still don't know."

"A special bodyguard, perhaps, considering the move against Alicia?"

"Possibly." Gutierrez didn't sound convinced.

"He's not with the police?" Castillo didn't have to feign the consternation in his voice this time.

Gutierrez shook his head. "Impossible. He killed three of my men at Exposition Park and ran away. No one downtown has heard of him."

"So then, an unknown quantity." Castillo hesitated, playing out the scene before he dropped the bomb. "I think it would be best if you stepped back a bit and handled some administrative matters for the next few days."

"Administrative matters?"

"Office work," Castillo said. "We have this stranger on the street whom you can't seem to find, and every time he meets your people, someone dies. Someone from our side, might I add. It isn't helping us, Ramon. I can't control the media if people keep dying."

"But—"

"My mind's made up," Castillo told him sternly. "I will still consult with you on strategy, of course, but for the moment it is best for all concerned if you—how do they say it in America—lay low."

"You're making a mistake," Gutierrez warned him, scowling.

"I'll take that chance."

"Havana—"

"Will of course correct me if I'm wrong. Feel free to call them through the normal channels."

That took some of the wind from Gutierrez's sails and set him to thinking. He nodded curtly, rose from his chair and moved toward the door. Halting at the threshold, he turned back toward Castillo, an unfamiliar worried look darkening his swarthy features.

"Armand, you'd tell me if there was something wrong?"

"Of course, my friend." Castillo's smile was genuine this time, enjoying the game. "You'd be the first to know."

The door swung behind Gutierrez, leaving the candidate alone.

Not bad, he thought. In fact, it had gone better than he dared to hope. Ramon would still bear watching, but that was expected. And if he stepped out of line, well, Havana would just have to understand that accidents happen.

They happen every day.

ERNO SOTO WAS halfway back to his apartment when he realized he had forgotten something at the office. Martin was expecting his assessment of the new opinion polls first thing the next day, and the paperwork was sitting on his desk in a manila envelope.

He cursed Gutierrez for distracting him and turned the car around. There was nothing to be done about it but retrace his route and pick the damned thing up. It meant another late night at the personal computer, but that was what Martin paid him for.

The very thought of Grandier forced a harsh laugh from Soto, braying in the silence of his compact car. No one suspected him of anything, the idiots. He was among the highest-ranking members of the team, trusted implicitly with every crucial secret of the campaign.

It was perfect.

Soto had hesitated for all of a day when Gutierrez approached him the first time, offering cash and other incentives for cooperation in undoing Grandier's cause. There was a pang of conscience at the outset, but self-interest had carried the day. When he compared his prospects in the Grandier administration, bound by laws and rules, to the potential for advancement under Armand Castillo, with all his lucrative contacts, it was finally no contest.

Soto was a modern individualist in the great Western tradition that Grandier claimed to espouse. Martin should be proud of him, in fact.

He was simply looking out for number one.

The rain was pelting down, and there was lightning now, with thunder riding on its coattails. He turned the switch that set his windshield wipers at a faster speed, but it was still a challenge driving in the downpour, water streaming down the glass on every side.

He slowed outside the campaign office, checked both ways as best he could with rain-streaked mirrors and his windows fogged over on the inside, and finally risked a U-turn in the middle of the street. He had a small umbrella, but the wind was such by now that he would still be soaked before he reached the doorway. Saving even half a dozen steps would make the effort that much less distasteful.

Soto had his mind fixed on a double whiskey and a long, hot shower as he stepped out of the car. The paperwork would keep him up past midnight, so there was no point rushing it. There would be time enough for sleeping later, when his work was done and he had reaped his various rewards.

He had his key in hand, already bending toward the lock, before he noticed there were lights on in the office. Not the main room, out in front, but somewhere at the back.

He hesitated, raindrops blowing in his face, and stared. Could it be coming from *his* office?

Soto knew that he had turned the lights off when he left
He was meticulous about such things. Whatever harm he
did to Martin Grandier's campaign through treachery, he
wouldn't be accused of bleeding the party treasury with
excessive utility bills.

He hesitated, frowning, finally let himself inside. Moving cautiously, trying to avoid the slightest sound, he
placed his umbrella on the floor without closing it, leaving the water to drip where it would. His shoes had leather
soles, and Soto thanked his lucky stars that he wasn't a fan
of the expensive jogging shoes that squeaked outra-
geously on vinyl floors whenever they got slightly damp.

It was his office, dammit! What the hell was going on?

He followed the light, taking care with each step, closing in on the cubicle he called his own, next door to Martin Grandier's slightly larger office. The door was standing
open, and he knew it had been closed before he left the
building.

Muffled sounds were emanating from the office, someone shuffling papers, searching. But for what?

A sudden rush of panic gripped him. They had found
him out! His treachery was known to Grandier, and they
were seeking evidence to trap him. There was nothing—he
wasn't that stupid—but the very fact that someone was
assigned to make the search told Soto all he had to know.

His run was over, scrapped before he had a chance to
reach the finish line. Gutierrez wouldn't pay him now. In
fact, Castillo's people would deny that he had ever served
them. It was part of the agreement going in.

He peered around the doorjamb, almost gasping at the
scene before his eyes. Alicia Grandier was rifling through
the top drawer of his filing cabinet, lifting out certain
folders, examining their contents briefly and returning
them to their appointed places.

His mind was racing now. What could he do to salvage
something from an evident disaster? When it hit him, the
sensation of relief was almost strong enough to take his
breath away.

Alicia had been missing since the brawl at Exposition Park. He knew that she had phoned her father's home to say that she was safe, but she hadn't been back in touch since then, as far as Soto was aware. He had no clear idea of how the woman had found him out—a hunch perhaps, or maybe she had been returning to the office on her own as he was huddled with Ramon outside, a stupid move at that. In any case, there was a possibility that she was acting on her own, without consulting her father.

If that was true, then Soto had a chance to save himself. Not only that, but he might turn a further profit on the deal.

He knew that the Colombians were looking for Alicia. Since the grim fiasco in the park, Gutierrez and his men had joined the hunt. If Soto could deliver her and simultaneously guard his own dark secret, why, so much the better.

It was really very simple when he thought about it. All he had to do was take her by surprise, subdue her somehow and deliver her to his employers.

Easy.

Still, the thought was one thing; putting it in action was a different game entirely.

Soto steeled himself and moved in on tiptoe, creeping up behind Alicia while her full attention was focused on the files. He could have laughed out loud, the stupid woman wasting time on paperwork that would have told her nothing if she looked all night. How stupid did she really think he was?

No matter.

He was close enough to touch her now, deciding whether he should grab her and risk a wrestling match or try to knock her out. Discretion was the better part of valor, and he reached back for a paperweight that occupied one corner of the desk, a Lucite globe in which a large black scorpion had been preserved, forever fresh.

Be careful now. A blow with too much force behind it could be fatal, while a gentle tap might fail to do the job. He was a novice at such things. Do it!

She was turning now, as if his urgent thought had somehow bridged the gap between them telepathically. She blinked at Soto in alarm, her left arm rising as he swung the paperweight against her skull. It was a sloppy job, glancing off her forehead, inches away from his intended target, but it drove Alicia back against the filing cabinet with sufficient force to slam the open drawer.

Her legs were buckling, and he swung again before she could recover from the shock of his assault. A better shot this time. He saw her eyes roll back, her mouth drop open as she slithered to the floor.

Unconscious? Faking? Dead?

He pressed two fingertips against her throat and felt a steady pulse. There was no physical response when he reached down to pinch her breast, and Soto reckoned she was truly out.

But for how long?

He was completely ignorant of such things, but he knew that she had to be restrained somehow before she came around. It wouldn't do for her to wake and attack him while he drove to the delivery point—wherever that might be.

There was no rope around the office, and he couldn't spare electric cord from any of the lamps or telephones. At last he settled for a roll of strapping tape they used on packages, securing Alicia's wrists behind her, ankles next, a final twist around her head to seal her lips.

All done.

The rain would cover his retreat, once he had finished cleaning up the office to erase any signs of struggle, but before that he would need advice. He reached across the desk and picked up the telephone receiver, punching out Ramon's home number.

Four rings before one of his flunkies answered.

"What?"

"I need Ramon," he blurted, feeling clammy perspiration soaking through his shirt. "It's an emergency."

MARTIN GRANDIER HAD BEEN reluctant to sit down with Bolan, but he finally agreed, as much from weariness as anything, the Executioner supposed. He wouldn't leave the house, considering that night's events, and Bolan didn't blame him. Calling from a phone booth half a mile from Grandier's retreat, he had anticipated dropping by.

In fact, it suited him just fine.

The bodyguards were waiting for him, and patted Bolan down. He let one of them pocket the Beretta, watching as another opened up his bag and blinked, his face a study in surprise.

An unexpected pile of currency will do that every time.

They let him keep the bag and passed him through, an escort front and back, conducting Bolan through the house to reach the den where Grandier was waiting, shadows etched beneath his eyes. If Bolan hadn't seen him hours earlier, he might have guessed the candidate was suffering from some degenerative illness, but instead he knew it was fatigue and worry. If the game went on much longer at its present pace, he thought that Grandier might be a victim of attrition, lost along the way.

"Please, have a seat." He was a gentleman in spite of everything.

They sat in matching easy chairs, a coffee table between them. Bolan placed his satchel on the table, nudging it toward Grandier. "A small donation to the cause," he said.

The candidate frowned as he took the heavy bag and placed it in his lap, then opened it and peered inside. His frown seemed carved in stone.

"This isn't small," Grandier commented, "but then you know that. I must ask you where it came from."

"Say I found it in the street."

"I'm sorry, that's not good enough. If it was sent by your employers..."

Bolan smiled and shook his head. "Not even close."

"Where, then?"

"You want the truth?"

"Of course."

"All right. A couple of Castillo's men decided it would be in their best interest to change sides. They can't go public, as it is, but money seemed to be the next best thing."

"May I assume you helped them to decide?"

"We had a little talk. They saw the light."

"Blood money," Grandier declared, placing the bag back on the coffee table. Neutral territory. No-man's-land.

"I used to feel that way myself," Bolan said. "Over time, though, I've decided money doesn't have a conscience. It's a tool and nothing more. Sometimes it's more important where a dollar goes than where it comes from."

"Once again, ends justify the means."

"Not quite," the Executioner replied. "This money comes from drugs, okay? If I had left it where I found it, someone would be spending it tomorrow on another cocaine shipment, maybe paying off corrupt policemen or a triggerman assigned to take you down. This way it goes to help your decent countrymen instead. I can't see any harm in that."

"There is a principle involved," Grandier said.

"Agreed. At home we have a confiscation program in effect for smugglers. The police can take their money, houses, cars, whatever. Sell it off and use the income to arrest more dealers, take more poison off the street. That way, the savages pick up at least a portion of the tab for all the misery they cause. I call that justice."

"We have no confiscation program in New Amsterdam," the candidate stated.

"Well, you can put it on your list of things to do once you're elected," Bolan said.

"The law requires that I report campaign donations."

"Fine by me. Is there something I should sign?"

Both men were smiling now, albeit grudgingly from Grandier. He recognized the obvious absurdity of having "Mike Belasko" sign a false name to a tax receipt, the whole scene weird enough to make him chuckle softly.

"This is very strange," he said at last.

"It keeps life interesting."

"My daughter called," Grandier said. "She's with your friend. I hope that she is safe."

"I trust him with my life," Bolan replied, meaning it. "He'll die before he lets her suffer any harm."

"There has been too much death already. This is supposed to be a free election, not a war."

"You didn't start the violence," Bolan said. "You're not responsible for what Castillo's people do, and you have no idea what I've been doing since the last time we sat down together. Any way you look at it, you're clean."

"Then why do I feel dirty?" Grandier inquired.

"Because you're an idealist. We need more like you, even if you sometimes get confused between reality and how things ought to be."

"You mean to say I'm living in a dreamworld."

"Dreamers have their place," Bolan said, "but they have to wake up now and then to keep the predators from sneaking up on them."

"I understand."

"It goes against the grain, though."

"Yes."

"When I was younger," Bolan told him, "I went to serve my country in a war that soon became unpopular. They're making movies now about my war, and people who weren't even born when I went off to fight are judging history by what comes out of Hollywood."

"Your point?"

"Times change. A little flexibility won't kill you, and it won't destroy your principles. The truth hangs in there if you give it half a chance."

"And this—" he pointed to the leather bag "—will help me spread the truth?"

"It might, at that."

"In that case, thank you."

"My pleasure," Bolan replied, already rising from his easy chair. "And now..."

"You have more work to do," said Grandier. It didn't come out sounding like a question.

"Right."

"Be careful, please."

"I will."

"Perhaps someday we'll both find peace."

And it was Bolan's turn to wonder, frowning. "Stranger things have happened, I suppose," he said, and turned away.

12

Alicia Grandier woke up to pain. It took her several moments to identify the different types and quantify each new sensation, but she seemed to have no other pressing business at the moment. With her hands and feet securely bound, she wasn't going anywhere.

The headache first. It filled her skull to bursting with a sick, dull throbbing, waves of nausea rippling through her body every time she moved. Two extratender areas denoted points of impact, and she pictured Erno Soto flailing at her, something round and heavy in his hand, a makeshift weapon.

Bastard!

She would make him pay for this as soon as she was able to escape.

The other pains were nothing in comparison to that inside her skull. The skin around her mouth felt raw, as if it had been rubbed with coarse sandpaper. When Alicia licked her lips, she tasted something rubbery. Some kind of tape?

Her wrists and ankles were secured with rope. It had the greasy feel of nylon line, and it was tight enough to threaten circulation without totally cutting off the flow of blood to her extremities. Alicia made a point of wiggling her toes and fingers every ten or fifteen minutes to make sure that they were functional.

Beyond the localized discomfort caused by some specific trauma, her whole body ached as if she had been squeezed into a box and left there overnight. A part of it was psychological, she thought, but Erno had to have carried her outside and placed her in his compact car—perhaps the trunk. She had recovered consciousness inside a small room, furnished only with a cot and single straight-backed wooden chair. How long the drive had been, she had no way of knowing, but it would account for stiffness in her muscles and a range of minor bruises, head to toe.

It was her own damned fault, at that. She should have known that Soto wouldn't keep incriminating papers at the office. In her zeal to punish him for selling out her father, she had turned her back on logic. Worst of all, she had proceeded hastily, without informing anyone of what she had discovered. No one else knew Soto was a traitor. If she simply disappeared...

But, no. It wouldn't be that easy.

If Castillo and his cronies wished her dead, they would have killed her while she lay unconscious, dumped her body where it would never be recovered. Let suspicion swirl around her father's enemies. Without some solid evidence, police would have no case.

The fact that she was still alive meant that her captors weren't finished with her yet. They had a reason for allowing her to live, and it could only be some new attack on her father, his campaign.

Belasko and Raul had tried to warn her earlier that day, but she refused to listen. They had said Castillo and his cronies would do anything within their power to secure a victory in the election. If Alicia was their hostage, they could dictate terms to Martin Grandier. He would be forced to quit the race, concede defeat.

Castillo would devise a subtle plan, of course. Nothing too obvious for the press or the authorities to run with. Sudden illness ought to cover it, the diagnosis left deliberately vague, but there were other ways around the problem, too. And later on, if Grandier had an "accident" well after the election, well, it would be written off as grim coincidence and nothing more.

And where would she be in the meantime?

Lying on the cot, bound hand and foot, Alicia knew that she would never be released alive. Her testimony in a court of law would link Ramon Gutierrez to her father's trusted aide, and that would mean significant embarrassment, at least, for Castillo. If Soto or Gutierrez started talking to police, Castillo would be next in line to occupy a prison cell.

No, they would never let her go.

The knowledge of her own impending death was strangely liberating. It transcended fear, instilled in Alicia a sense that she had nothing left to lose. Whatever happened next, she could resist her captors, knowing that their promises of freedom in return for her cooperation would be lies.

Her fate was sealed. The only thing she could accomplish through surrender was the ruin of her father and delivery of her homeland to the enemy.

Her thoughts went back to Raul Camacho, and she felt a sudden rush of hope. Was there a chance that he could find her even now? When he discovered she had left the safehouse, would he try to seek her out? The first stop logically would be her father's house, and failing there, Alicia's own apartment. He would get back to the campaign office, given time... but what would he discover there?

Precisely nothing.

Erno Soto was above suspicion in her father's eyes, and there was nothing in the office to incriminate him. Raul would surely think that she had been abducted off the street. He would go looking for Gutierrez and the Obregons, perhaps Castillo. Was it possible that he would find her after all? Before it was too late?

As if in answer to her silent thoughts, she heard a sound of heavy footsteps in the corridor outside her Spartan cell. Another moment, and the door swung open to admit Ramon Gutierrez. He was smiling, towering above her like a giant as she lay there on the cot.

"We need to have a little talk," he said, and slowly closed the door.

"YOU MISSED YOUR FRIEND," a sullen bodyguard told Rafael Encizo as he left his car and walked toward the house. His Smith & Wesson Model 411 was beneath the driver's seat, and so the frisk found nothing that would stop his passing on.

Inside the house there was an atmosphere of gloom that put Encizo on alert. His instinct told him that it had to be more than a delayed reaction to the brawl at Exposition Park and Grandier's interrogation by police. The tension here was palpable, a living thing that tried to wrap itself around him as he entered. Only with an effort did he shake it off as he moved on in search of Martin Grandier.

And found him in the study, under guard. The candidate glanced up and seemed to brighten for an instant, but the moment faded quickly and he slumped back in his chair. A listless wave dispatched his watchdogs to a station in the hall, and Encizo closed the door behind him, moving toward a chair.

"My daughter," Grandier began before Encizo had a chance to ask the question. "They have taken my Alicia. First I thought she was with you, but now I see . . ."

The sentence trailed off, incomplete. Encizo felt a cold chill rippling down his back.

"Who told you this?" he asked.

"A man called about twenty minutes ago," Grandier replied. "At first I thought he had to be lying, but he put Alicia on the line. She told me to ignore his threats. I heard him strike her."

"Did you recognize the caller's voice?" Encizo asked.

Grandier shook his head. "I think it was Gutierrez, but I can't be sure. He has no shortage of assistants who would shield him."

"They can always try," Encizo said. His voice was as cold as ice, hard enough to cut glass.

"What are you thinking?"

"Nothing yet. There were demands?"

"Of course. I should retire from the campaign and offer some excuse about my health. He left the details up to

e. If I do not comply by noon tomorrow, they will send licia back to me ... one piece at a time."

Tears coursed down Grandier's cheeks as he spoke. Encizo realized there was as much frustrated anger in the candidate's response as there was guilt and fear for what might happen to his daughter if he didn't quit the race.

"Before you cave in," Encizo said, "you should know they'll never let her go alive."

Grandier blinked at that, lifting his face. Fear instantly eclipsed his other visible expressions. "What? Why not?"

"Because she must know who they are," Encizo replied. "No matter what you promise them, no matter what he says, they can't allow a witness to survive. Where would they be if they release her and she goes to the police?"

"My God, it's hopeless, then."

"Not quite."

"But how ...?"

"When I was coming in just now, one of your people told me Mike Belasko paid a visit earlier."

"That's true. He brought a contribution for the party. won't need it now."

"Don't fold your hand just yet. Did he say anything about his plans? Where he was going?"

"Nothing that would help you find him," Grandier replied. "I gathered that he planned to cause more trouble for the Obregons."

"I wouldn't be surprised."

Encizo's mind was racing now. He would be forced to leave another message on the cutout answering machine, and that meant waiting for the Executioner to check back in. It would be fruitless trying to find Bolan in Hollandia when he was on the move. And yet Encizo couldn't bear the thought of sitting still and doing nothing while Alicia was in savage hands.

"We have a number," he told Grandier, "where I can leave a message in emergencies. I'll call and put your number on the tape. When he calls back, I want you to

explain what's happened. He can help you. In the mear
time, I'll be looking for Alicia on my own.''

"But how?"

"Don't ask, unless you really want to know."

The answer must have been in his eyes, for Grandie
blinked twice and turned away. His voice, when he bega
to speak at last, was barely audible, a whisper from th
bottom of a well.

"Do anything you must," he said, a tremor in his ton
"Please bring her back to me. She's all I have."

It was time for total honesty. "No guarantees," Enciz
said, "but I can promise you one thing—the bastards wi
regret this move until the day they die."

And he stopped short of adding that once Mack Bola
got involved, that day wouldn't be far removed.

"It never should have come to this," Grandier said.

"It wasn't your choice," Encizo reminded him. "If th
opposition wants to play with fire, they're going to g
burned."

The candidate made no response to that, his face turne
toward the window, where a steady sheet of wind-lashe
rain was beating at the glass. Encizo rose and crossed th
room to reach the nearest telephone. In less than thirt
seconds, he had left his message on the tape for Bolan t
retrieve when he found time.

And time, the Cuban realized, was one thing they didn'
possess in any great supply.

ERNO SOTO HAD BEEN CALLED at home immediately afte
Martin Grandier received the message that his daughte
was a prisoner. The ultimatum had included warnings n
to speak with the authorities, but Grandier was calling i
his trusted aides, as if a show of strength around the hous
would somehow bring Alicia home unharmed.

Small chance of that, the turncoat thought. In fact, n
chance at all. The woman was as good as dead the mo
ment he had found her sifting through his files. Gutierre
might amuse himself by keeping her alive until her usefu
ness had passed, but that would be the end of it. A wi

ess was the last thing any of them needed at the moment,
nd Ramon was a professional at solving problems of the
uman kind.

There had been no way Soto could decline the sum-
nons from his boss. It was impossible for him to stay
way, but he had dawdled over changing clothes and
riven slowly through the pouring rain. As he arrived
utside the house, he had seen Raul Camacho leaving,
unning to his car.

Goddammit!

He was under orders to alert Ramon the next time he
rossed paths with the mysterious Camacho, but he
ouldn't do it now. The guards outside had seen his car,
nd one of them was waving him into the curbside space
Camacho left behind. If Soto drove away now without
topping, it would certainly arouse suspicion.

No, he had to go inside and play his part without a slip-
p. If he had a chance to phone Gutierrez from the house,
nen he would do so. Otherwise, what Ramon didn't know
vouldn't hurt him.

Meanwhile, Soto had to concentrate on looking out for
umber one.

He parked his car and reached for his umbrella, swal-
owing a nauseating wave of apprehension as he thought
f Martin Grandier. Of course, the man didn't suspect him
f complicity in Alicia's abduction. How could he? No one
ad seen them together at the office, and there had been no
me for Alicia to confide her suspicions to anyone else.
he bodyguards would surely not be nodding at him now
he was suspected of placing the candidate's daughter in
nemy hands.

So far, so good.

Inside the house he found the staff subdued, a couple of
ne women weeping softly as they sat together on a sofa in
ne living room. He was reminded of a funeral parlor, rel-
tives convened to see a late, lamented loved one on his
ay.

Soto brushed past another pair of bodyguards, one of
nem armed, his pistol too late and too little to make any

difference. The campaign was already finished, wheth
these sorry fools knew it or not. The end had come fo
Martin Grandier when Soto found his daughter poking h
long nose in where it didn't belong.

So be it.

He felt no remorse for what had happened—what wou
happen—to the woman. It was her fault, meddling in h
private business, getting caught that way. His only appre
hension centered on the possibility that he might still b
linked to her removal somehow, through some mecha
nism he hadn't considered previously. If that hap
pened ...

What? How could he save himself? What would he do

Betray Gutierrez, certainly, if that would buy him l
niency. Soto could worry about the rest of it, reprisa
from the Cubans, at some later date. Ideally though, b
would avoid detection altogether, cling to Grandier as
trusted confidante until the bitter end.

And after that, what then?

There was Castillo, holding out the promise of a lucr
tive position in his new administration once the final vot
were cast. There would be obvious recriminations from h
friends, but that was simply politics. How many offic
holders in the States had changed affiliations, sometime
more than once, before they got it right?

The money was another matter altogether. He ha
banked it in the Cayman Islands, waiting for the day whe
he could bring it home under the new regime, a financi
drop in the bucket compared to all the drug money Ca
tillo would be moving through New Amsterdam. So
thought he might even ask Armand for an introduction
the Obregon brothers, invest in a shipment or two ar
make himself some real money on the side.

He saw Alicia in his mind's eye, knowing that her li
would be the price of his advancement, and he didn't car
The thought had troubled him a bit in abstract terms, whi
he was on his way to meet Gutierrez, but ambition was tl
touchstone of his life. Whatever benefited Erno Soto, b

would do it given half a chance and justify the action later to himself.

He made his way along the corridor to Martin's study, a familiar path that he had followed countless times before. The door was standing open, muffled voices emanating from within. He peeked around the corner and found the candidate discussing something with his secretary.

Soto waited.

When the woman came out moments later, he moved in to take her place. Grandier stood to greet him, crossing the carpet with outstretched arms. The embrace was fervent, almost passionate. He saw and felt that Martin's cheeks were moist from crying.

"Is there anything that I can do?" the traitor asked.

MACK BOLAN CAUGHT Encizo's message forty minutes after it was left, called Martin Grandier at once, and felt his anger mounting as he listened to the details of Alicia's disappearance, the phone call, the ultimatum from their common enemy.

"The deadline's noon," he said when Grandier had finished pouring out his fears. "I hope you won't make any statement to the press before that time. It's possible that I can help you."

"That is what your friend said, too."

"Raul?"

"He left here shortly after calling you. I don't know where he's gone."

The Executioner could guess, though not specifically. They had a list of targets in Hollandia, the suburbs and surrounding countryside. Encizo knew his methods, knew how Bolan would react to the abduction. If he got a jump on Bolan this time, rattling the opposition's cage, so much the better.

Two warriors working independently could cover twice the ground of one. The damage they inflicted on their en-

emy would more than double if they played their cards
right and avoided running into each other.

The police scanner would help him there, Bolan
thought. He could keep track of the latest action by
eavesdropping on official bulletins, avoid the targets chosen by his friend. Somewhere along the line, with any luck
at all, they would touch base, coordinate their strategy for
optimum results.

All bets were off from this point forward. If they had
avoided stepping on Armand Castillo's toes before, that
was about to change. No one would be immune from the
new heat coming down on Hollandia, as far as Bolan was
concerned.

His strategy for freeing hostages was simple: make the
lives of the abductors so unbearable that they would scrub
their plans, do anything at all to save themselves from
further punishment. There was a risk, of course, whenever lives were riding on the line. Alicia's captors might
decide that it was easier to kill her and retreat than risk releasing her alive.

In that case, there would be no mercy when he tracked
them down, and nothing would prevent him from pursu-
ing them—around the globe, if necessary—to exact revenge.

The voice of Martin Grandier brought Bolan back to the
here and now.

"What can you do?" the candidate was asking. "Is
there any hope?"

"There's always hope," Bolan replied, "but I'd be a liar
if I made you any promises."

"Your friend said that, as well."

Encizo knew what he was doing. He would never snow
the lady's kin with false assurances that he could guarantee a happy ending. Any promise, in a case like this, boiled
down to wishful thinking, and the guilt of building up false
hopes could drag a soldier down, prevent him from responding promptly and appropriately when his full attention was demanded on the battlefield.

"I have to go now," Bolan said to Grandier. "I'll be in touch when I have something to report. Meantime, stay where you are and don't say anything about this to the media."

"I understand. My daughter's fate is in your hands."

"Not quite," the Executioner corrected him, "but I'll do what I can to bring her home."

"Goodbye."

There was a grim note of finality in Grandier's voice as he broke the connection, almost as if he regarded Bolan's mission as futile. Maybe it was better, the warrior thought, to face the worst and make your peace with pain before it really hit you. It was sometimes easier to cope with grief that way... or so he had been told.

Except, he realized, there was no easy way to lose a loved one. Any way you sliced it, there was pain and suffering enough to go around.

This time, at least, he meant to pass those negative reactions onward to the men responsible—the Obregons, Armand Castillo and his bullyboys provided by the DGI. He didn't know which faction of the opposition party had Alicia, who had given orders for the snatch, and he wasn't much interested in finding out. When he began to beat the bushes, raising hell with anyone connected to Castillo, word would get around.

And someone, somewhere in Hollandia, would get the message.

From that point it came down to their response.

If they released Alicia unharmed, the Executioner could find it in his heart to make a deal. Allow some lead time for his enemies to fold their tents and leave New Amsterdam. But if they took a hard line, kept her locked away or killed her...

His thoughts inevitably turned to other hostages and other killing grounds. How often had he played this game before, with innocent flesh riding on the line?

Too often.

Still, the minds of Bolan's enemies ran in a certain groove. They lived by terrorism and intimidation, forcing their will on the helpless and frightened until someone came along and made them stop. More often than not, the only thing that finally stopped them was a bullet.

Right now the Executioner had bullets to spare.

13

The slaughterhouse, a half mile due east of Hollandia, had closed its doors in 1967. After more than thirty years of butchery, the place was closed by rising debts and competition from a newer, more effective killing plant in Cranetown, twelve miles north along the coast.

Still, it took more than yanking out conveyor belts and hosing down the floors to purge a slaughterhouse of the pervasive death smell that had crept into the very walls, corrupting the whole atmosphere.

The latest tenants didn't seem to mind the smell.

The past two years Francisco Obregon had owned the property, employed it as a combination warehouse, operations center and staging area for the troops he imported to safeguard his growing empire on New Amsterdam. The place was not a cutting plant per se, but drugs were sometimes left there for a day or two, in transit, under heavy guard. At other times the slaughterhouse was useful as a makeshift barracks, for interrogations, an elimination now and then.

Francisco reckoned that a little extra blood wouldn't be noticed in the circumstances. He enjoyed his privacy, and while the boss himself would never deign to sleep within those walls, the place was good enough for his subordinates.

Encizo knew the slaughterhouse by reputation, as a target on the list prepared by Stony Man so long ago. It felt like weeks or months since he had landed on New Amsterdam. So much had happened since his plane touched down, so many men had died—and now he was about to put a few more numbers on the scorecard.

The rain and darkness covered his approach. Encizo wore plastic goggles to protect his eyes from wind and raindrops, paying no attention to the sopping-wet fatigues, a clammy second skin. It was a short jog from his car, the weapons tough enough to stand a little rain and still perform upon command.

He had retrieved an MP-5 K submachine gun from the stash he shared with Bolan, adding a Beretta 92-F to the captured Smith & Wesson automatic he already had. With extra magazines for the Beretta and the SMG, he felt a bit more confident about the odds. He had no fix on numbers for the enemy, but four cars were parked around the east side of the one-time slaughterhouse.

At least that many then. More likely eight or nine. Perhaps as many as sixteen.

Those would be killer odds, but he was going in regardless.

For Alicia.

Entry was a relatively simple matter, working on a side door with his knife, stepping into semidarkness once he beat the ancient lock. Ahead of him faint lights were burning around a corner leading to the main room of the slaughterhouse. No one was there when Encizo checked out the spacious killing room.

Upstairs, then.

Following his instinct and his nose, he mounted two flights of steps to reach the second floor, the smell of something spicy growing stronger with each step. On the second floor the space had been divided by partitions into office space and storage, little in the way of furnishings these days to tell him which was which.

Not that he cared.

A right turn took him to the makeshift kitchen, where three camp stoves were laid out on a table, end to end. On two of them pots were simmering, giving off aromas that made the Cuban's mouth water, but he put the thought of food aside, concentrating on the soldiers ranged in front of him.

There were five men, all young, in casual attire. Four of them sported shoulder holsters, while the fifth preferred to wear his side arm in a cross-draw holster on his left.

The "sporting" thing would probably have been for Encizo to call out his targets, let one of them draw first, but this was real life, not the movies. In a showdown, when your life was on the line, you made full use of any small advantages that came your way.

Surprise, for instance.

Two steps put him in the kitchen, and his SMG was stuttering before he crossed the threshold, raking left to right. The first two gunners never knew what hit them, crimson spouting from their backs as parabellum manglers shredded flesh and fabric and sent them down together in a lifeless sprawl. The third man had begun to turn, not reaching for his weapon yet, and Encizo depressed the muzzle of his weapon, shattering the *pistolero*'s kneecaps with a well-placed burst.

He would be needing someone who could talk, if all went well.

The last two shooters had time enough to reach their weapons, but responding with a decent shot was something else. Encizo caught the fourth man as he turned, a shiny autoloader in his hand, and stitched a ragged line of holes across his chest. The guy went over backward, snarling like a wounded animal, but silent once he was stretched out on the floor.

And that left one.

The final gunner fired two hasty shots, and both of them flew wide. Encizo used the last rounds in his magazine to slam his target backward, pinning him against the nearest wall. The dead man left a streak of crimson as his legs collapsed and let him slither to the floor.

Reloading swiftly, the Phoenix Force warrior stood listening for the sound of voices, hurried footsteps, something that would lead him to another target. There was nothing, but he let another moment pass, still listening, before he made his move.

He knelt beside the wounded gunner, took the side arm from his shoulder holster and flung it toward the far side of the room. The weapon generated a sharp metallic clatter as it hit the concrete floor and slid for several yards.

The *pistolero* had both hands clasped to his ruined kneecaps, staring up at Encizo through eyes that brimmed with tears of pain. He tried to squirm away, but there was nowhere he could go, no place to hide. At last, resigned, he waited for the ax to fall.

Instead of shooting him between the eyes, Encizo spoke to him in Spanish. "Can you hear me?"

"Yes."

"Your mind is clear? You understand?"

"I hear you."

It was close enough.

"I have a message for Francisco Obregon," Encizo said. "You promise to deliver it, and I'll let you live."

The gunner thought about it for a heartbeat, grimacing at another wave of agony erupting from his shattered limbs, and nodded.

"Yes."

"I want the girl. I'm turning up the heat until Francisco lets her go unharmed. He won't get any better deals in town. He ought to think about it, understand?"

"A girl?" Even through his pain, the gunner was confused.

"It's not your problem," Encizo informed him. "You just pass the message, okay?"

"This girl, you want her back."

"Unharmed, I said."

"No harm."

"Can you remember that?"

The gunner nodded.

"So live," Encizo said, and put that place behind him, moving toward another target on his list.

ARMAND CASTILLO'S campaign headquarters was brightly
t inside, despite the hour. Bolan could see half a dozen
aen from where he sat across the street, but no women.
'rom the look of things it would be strictly stag tonight, a
athering of muscle to defend the cause.

Bolan had refrained from hassling Castillo's people un-
l now, and he still had no intention of attacking cam-
aign volunteers per se. But Armand's hardforce was a
ifferent story. The Executioner understood that some of
1em were DGI, the rest a group of local thugs recruited to
arass and terrorize supporters of the Grandier cam-
aign. A few of them were known by name to agents of the
)EA, and each possessed a lengthy rap sheet, with of-
:nses ranging from assault to robbery, manslaughter, ar-
on, rape.

They were the dregs of a society attempting to evolve,
:make itself into a workable democracy. No one would
1iss them if they suffered lethal accidents tonight or
ometime in the future.

Their loss, Bolan thought, was New Amsterdam's gain.

He thought about the front door, scratched it off his list
nd drove around in back. The alley offered him a better
ngle of attack, no windows to permit the opposition any
varning. If he didn't have to blow the back door going in,
e could achieve complete surprise.

He took the Mini-Uzi with its custom silencer and
lipped it underneath his raincoat. Extra magazines rode
eavy in his pockets as he stepped out of the car into a
riving rain. He reached the door in three long strides,
:ached out to test the knob and felt it turn.

The troops were getting sloppy. Few of them had been
:quired to fight since Bolan launched his campaign in
[ew Amsterdam, and roughly half of those were dead, the
thers convalescing from their injuries. This crew was
resh and cocky with the average criminal's contempt for
anger that didn't appear immediate. If someone out there
ad a hard-on for the Obregons, what of it? Playing sen-
ry was a lark, as long as there was no one out there in the
arkness waiting to attack.

The back door opened on a smallish storage room, yellow light spilling into the alley as Bolan entered. On his right a beefy punk was dozing in a metal folding chair cocked back against the wall, his first intimation of danger a wet breeze gusting through the open doorway.

Waking too late, the gunner tried to reach a pistol underneath his sport coat. Bolan raised the Mini-Uzi, stroked the trigger lightly for a silent three-round burst and took the shooter's face off, spattering gray-and-crimson abstract patterns on the wall behind him.

He cleared the storage room before the folding chair collapsed and dropped its lifeless burden on the floor. In front of him a narrow hallway led toward the street, with doorless office cubicles on either side. The first two offices were unoccupied, but he caught a sound of voices from the next room on his left.

He was approaching that door when a gunner in the front room spotted him and shouted an alarm to his companions. Bolan raised the Mini-Uzi, fired one-handed, and the lookout went down kicking.

His fall confused the others long enough for Bolan to deal with the two men in the office on his left. He poked his head and weapon through the open door, already firing as the two of them glanced up and saw grim death intruding on their private space. One sat at a desk with the other standing over him but neither one had time to reach a weapon as the stream of parabellum shockers dropped them in their tracks.

It was pandemonium out front, at least five voices shouting curses, questions, no one seemingly in charge. Bolan headed in that direction, moving in a combat crouch, acutely conscious of the bright fluorescents overhead.

A gunman stepped into his line of fire, his hand wrapped around an automatic pistol, and squeezed off three shots in rapid fire before he even had a chance to find his mark. It was a close thing even so, the bullets whispering past Bolan's face with only a foot to spare.

The Uzi answered with its muffled voice, like papers rustling in the wind, and Bolan watched his adversary stagger, leaking blood from a line of holes strung out across his chest and stomach. Gravity took over as the gunman rocked back on his heels, and in another second he was down, unmoving on the floor.

The Executioner had eliminated two of the original half dozen plus three more whom he hadn't seen from the street. That left a minimum of four targets, and he wouldn't have been surprised to learn that there were others somewhere on the premises.

But first things first.

He edged along the hallway, leading with the Uzi, prepared for anything. Someone was firing from the front room aimlessly, the bullets peppering the wall a few yards in front of Bolan, on his right. It was a wasted effort and he left them to it. Any bullets spent on walls and furniture were rounds he didn't have to think about when it was time to make his move.

He fished inside the left-hand pocket of his raincoat, came out with a frag grenade and pulled the safety pin. It would be almost hopeless, trying for a kill when he couldn't see any of his targets, but the Executioner was looking for a suitable diversion that would keep their heads down long enough to let him clear the last few yards of hallway.

If he killed or wounded some of his opponents in the process, that was fine, a small fringe benefit.

He lobbed the deadly egg left-handed, saw it strike the floor and wobble out of view around the corner to his right. A warning cry went up, but there was little to be done with a five-second fuse. Still, scuffling feet were audible before the blast that shattered windows and left his own ears ringing.

He charged across the intervening space and hit the threshold of the front room in a flying shoulder roll. Someone snapped shots at him on the left, and Bolan fired in that direction, spending the remainder of the Uzi's load before he came to rest behind a heavy wood-and-metal desk.

As the warrior reloaded quickly, he checked out the damage caused by the grenade. One man was down, blood flowing from a ragged scalp wound, seeping through the fabric of his slacks from other hidden injuries. He didn't move and Bolan put him out of mind, concentrating on second gunman, who staggered from his place behind filing cabinet.

The guy was dazed if nothing else, but he was also armed, a stubby riot shotgun held in front of him, his finger on the trigger. He was blinking at the smoke and dust that swirled around him, looking for a target. Another heartbeat and he would have found it, but his luck and time ran out as Bolan stroked the Uzi's trigger, rattling off a short precision burst.

The gunner did a jerky little two-step, sat down hard and slowly toppled over on his side. He lost the shotgun somewhere in the middle of his fall, and lay unmoving in spreading pool of blood, his eyes locked open, staring back at Bolan from beyond the void of death.

The gunners at his back, unfazed by the grenade blast were rushing now. He heard them coming and turned to meet them, lying prone behind the desk. Their legs were visible at once, and Bolan took the best shot he could manage, dropping both of them across his line of fire. The Mini-Uzi kept on stuttering, and in another heartbeat both of them lay still, blood mingling on the vinyl floor.

The rain was blowing in through the shattered window that faced the street. Bolan was rising from his crouch when something caught his ear, a new sound in the ringing silence after combat.

Someone was sobbing, the muffled noises emanating from beyond the point where Bolan's last two kills lay stretched out on the floor. He tracked the sound until he stood outside a door that bore the graphic symbols of a rest room meant for either sex. The weeping noise came from inside.

He took a chance and threw the door back, dropping to one knee and ready with the submachine gun as he did so. Huddled in the space between the toilet and the wall was a young man, both hands raised to protect himself; as if the flesh and bone would slow a bullet down.

"Speak English?" Bolan asked him.

"Yes."

"If you want to live, you've got one chance."

The young man blinked and bit off his sobbing, making sure he got it right the first time. "What?"

"I need an errand boy. Can you remember something? Tell it to your boss?"

"Yes, sir."

"I want the girl back," Bolan told him. "That's the message. Someone has her, and I want her back alive. Make sure Castillo understands."

"Castillo?"

"You're his muscle, aren't you?"

"I work for Ramon Gutierrez."

"Fine. Tell him, then. He can pass it on. Can you remember that?"

"You want a girl."

"*The* girl. Alive and kicking. Are we clear?"

"Yes, sir."

The warrior put that place behind him, searching for new prey.

IT WAS A ZOO out there, Pablo Obregon thought. Since breakfast everything that they had worked for in the past twelve months started to unravel, coming apart like wet tissue paper before his very eyes. Worse yet, he didn't have a clue who was responsible for the attacks that had already cost him . . . what? How many men?

He didn't want to think about the numbers. They would soon be running short of troops—he knew that much for certain. More were flying in from Medellín, but that took time. They had to pack and catch the plane, kill time at immigration once they reached New Amsterdam. Francisco had a fix in with a couple of the customs men to pass their bags—no search for weapons this time—but it cost a fortune, and he still had fears about a couple of the gunners getting stuck at passport control.

They were traveling on phony paperwork, but still, with their records in Colombia, it was possible that one or more would be recognized, detained for extradition on a list of pending warrants.

Damn. How had they come to this?

He thought about the taunting phone call from the stranger who was clearly an American, the man who had destroyed his office, killing three of Pablo's subordinates in front of him and making him grovel on the floor.

Someone would have to pay for that, and he was looking forward to the moment when he laid eyes on his unknown enemy. It would be good to turn the game around, take action for a change, instead of simply hiding and reacting to the blows that fell around him.

Pablo Obregon was sick and tired of running, hiding out. He was a man, goddammit! He was used to taking what he wanted and to hell with any consequences. Money, guns and high-priced lawyers kept him safe from harm, and he wouldn't be treated like some peasant from the hinterlands, harassed and terrorized.

It was bad enough that he had been forced to hide out in this small apartment in downtown Hollandia, away from his home and the luxuries he enjoyed as a mark of his authority in the cartel. It gave him claustrophobia, this eight-by-thirteen bedroom, beige paint on the walls and ceiling, threadbare carpet underfoot. Supposedly it was the best his men could do on such short notice, but Pablo wasn't convinced.

There had to be something better for a man of his importance, even in a pinch.

He missed the first shots altogether, wrapped up as he was in himself, but the familiar crash of breaking glass brought Pablo bolting from his rumpled bed, a pistol in his hand. Outside, from the direction of the living room, his men were firing now—three guns, a fourth. And what about the others? Where were they?

There was no time for wondering. His bedroom had no windows, in the interest of security, which meant that there was also no escape hatch. He could either risk the door, with bullets slapping all around it, or he could find himself a place to hide.

The bathroom? No, too obvious.

He thought of crawling underneath the bed, and stopped himself, a dark scowl on his face. It conjured painful memories of childhood, when he'd hidden from his drunken father, and besides, he doubted there was room enough for him beneath the sagging box spring.

To the closet then, without delay. There seemed to be no other choice.

He crossed the room in four long strides and ducked inside the musty-smelling closet, closing the door behind him. He felt in the darkness for a lock, but found none. Of course not. Who would put a lock inside a closet?

He scooted back into the farthest corner, braced his pistol in front of him in a tight two-handed grip, his elbows firmly planted on his knees. If anyone came looking for him here, he'd deal out sudden death.

The sound of gunfire from the living room had ceased, and Pablo waited, listening to footsteps on the creaky wooden floor. Someone had reached the bedroom threshold, tried the knob and found the door unlocked. The footsteps were in the bedroom now, crossing to the bathroom and peering inside, hunting him like an animal.

Pablo heard the footsteps coming back now, toward the closet, and he couldn't wait a moment longer. Cursing, he squeezed off four quick shots, fingers of light lancing into the closet through his bullet holes.

The response was immediate and terrifying.

No sooner was his final bullet on its way than an answering swarm began to rip the closet door to pieces, starting at the top and working downward in a rough zigzag pattern. A submachine gun with a silencer attached chewed up the door and peppered the wall behind him. In another instant it would have him, tearing him apart.

And then the shooting stopped. A graveyard voice addressed him from the bedroom.

"One chance, Pablo," the Executioner warned. "You can die in there or live awhile. Your choice. You want to live, I'll need the gun."

He thought about it, cursing underneath his breath. To be or not to be?

The dealer made his choice and tossed the pistol out.

"I'm coming, dammit! Just don't shoot."

14

Francisco Obregon was dozing when the houseman came to get him, nervous looking, with a strange expression on his face. At first the dealer was confused, disoriented, but it was a definite relief to find himself alive and whole, escaping from his dream.

His nightmare.

In the dream-scape he was running from a hulking, faceless shadow figure. That was bad enough, the running part, but he was wounded, too. One of his arms hung limp and useless at his side, and he could feel his strength draining from other wounds, seeping away with the blood that flowed from his chest and side. Behind him heavy footsteps were gaining fast, already loud enough to shake the earth beneath his feet.

And laughter.

When he glanced off to the left or right, Francisco saw the faces of a hundred different men he had eliminated on his rise to power. Dead and gone, they had returned somehow to witness his destruction, and the zombie bastards were delighted, laughing at him, making him the fool.

"What is it?" There was anger in his tone, held over from the nightmare, and his houseman flinched.

"The telephone." He seemed reluctant to say more.

"You want to tell me who it is, or should I guess?"

"Your brother, sir."

"Pablo?"

"Yes."

"What does he want?" Obregon asked, coming back to the matter at hand.

The houseman shrugged, becoming more uneasy by the moment. "He didn't tell me, sir. Says he needs to speak with you right now."

He gave up trying to interpret the houseman's weird expression, rising from the sofa and moving toward the nearby desk. His private telephone was silent, with a flashing light in place of the traditional bell tone. His staff screened all the calls, but he could still keep track of incoming messages and eavesdrop if he felt the urge.

The houseman left him, Obregon waiting for the door to close before he lifted the receiver to his ear. "Hello?"

"Hello, Francisco."

Shit! It wasn't Pablo's voice at all. He was about to slam down the phone, when the caller said, "Your brother says hello."

"Where is he?" Short hairs stirred on his nape.

"He's lying down right now. Rough night for Pablo. Send a couple of your men to check his crash pad, and you'll find out what I mean."

"Who is this?"

"Someone who's concerned about your family, Francisco. You've been going off the deep end lately, taking chances. Picking up Alicia Grandier like that, you made a serious mistake."

"You smokin' something funny, man. I didn't pick up nobody."

"Hey, my mistake. Thing is, since you're the man behind Castillo, you can take the heat, regardless. See the way it works?"

"I don't know what the fuck—"

"So listen up and learn."

The voice had taken on a steely edge, demanding full attention. Obregon bit off the first retort that came to mind and waited, listening.

"That's better. Now, your brother's life expectancy is linked directly to the woman's, got it? Anything your people or Castillo's do to her, I take it out on him, with interest. When he's all used up, I'm coming after you.''

"Why don't you do that now instead of playing games?"

"You think I'm playing here? Somebody told Alicia's father they'd be mailing her in pieces if he didn't quit the race by noon tomorrow. How about I send you something? Say, a little bit of Pablo for your mantelpiece. I'm sure we can agree on something that he wouldn't miss.''

"How do I know you've even got him?" Obregon demanded.

"He was talking to your gofer, but he got a little frisky, and I had to lay him out. He's napping as we speak. I couldn't promise you he's having pleasant dreams."

"I need some proof."

"For what? You tell me you don't have the woman— what's the difference?''

"I can find her, dammit! Someone grabbed her in Hollandia, I put the word out. We get answers pretty fast.''

"I hope so, for your brother's sake."

"The proof," Obregon prompted.

"You check his flat. Be careful, though. The cops will be there now, and I don't want you getting busted while you've still got work to do. If that doesn't satisfy you, I can send his pinkie in the morning mail. Get one of your *comrades* on the force to check the print.''

"You bastard."

"That's exactly right. Keep that in mind before you try to screw me, Frankie.''

"Suppose I have a problem with the woman?"

"Then your brother has a problem. Simple."

"What I'm telling you, since I don't have her, is that maybe by the time I find out where she's at, she's not in good shape anymore. You understand?''

"I guess you'd better keep your fingers crossed," the caller told him, his voice as cold as ice. "Maybe light a candle.''

"Hey—"

"No bullshit, Frankie. No excuses. You want Pablo back with all of his equipment functional, do what you have to do."

"How do I get in touch with you?"

"You don't. I'll call you back at eight o'clock. I hope you didn't plan on sleeping in."

"I'll be here."

"In the meantime I'll be visiting a few more of your operations just to let you know I'm serious."

"Hey, man—"

But he was talking to a dead line now, the dial tone buzzing in his ear. Francisco slammed down the telephone receiver, then picked it up and slammed it down again. He bellowed for the houseman, turning on him with a face that could have curdled milk.

"You told me that was Pablo on the line," he said.

"Yes, sir."

"And you're sure about that? There was no mistake?"

The houseman looked bewildered. "No mistake. I know his voice. He tells me 'This is Pablo, put my brother on the line.' I came and got you, like he said."

"All right. Get out of here."

The move against Alicia Grandier had been Francisco's brainstorm, but it had been scuttled earlier that day, four of his soldiers wasted on the street. Since then, he had been taking heavy punches and reeling from the shock. He had no time or opportunity to mount another snatch.

But someone had succeeded where Francisco's troops had failed.

Gutierrez?

It was worth a look, if nothing else. Ramon might have the woman tucked away somewhere, and if he didn't, there was still a chance that he had information on her whereabouts. Another player in the game, perhaps. The damned Cubans, with their talent for intrigue.

Whatever, she wasn't worth Pablo's life. Francisco meant to have his brother back at any cost, and once that was accomplished, he could set his mind to punishing the man or men responsible for his embarrassment.

ENCIZO VOLUNTEERED to baby-sit Pablo Obregon while Bolan made the rounds and lit a few more bonfires in Hollandia. He promised not to damage the Colombian unnecessarily, and the warrior trusted him to keep his word, despite the evident contempt he felt for Obregon. There was a personal edge to Encizo's attitude, but Bolan was disinclined to question it at the moment.

He had his hands full as well, just rattling the opposition's cage.

Next up, a shock to keep Francisco on his toes.

He saw the convoy coming from a quarter-mile away, four crew wagons running in tandem, their headlights knifing through the rain-streaked darkness. They were rolling in response to his conversation with Francisco, coming to check Pablo's crash pad, and Bolan meant to give them a surprise.

The MM-1 multiround projectile launcher was a specialty item, resembling an old-fashioned tommy gun on steroids, with its 12-round revolving cylinder and forward pistol grip. Instead of standard ammunition, though, it was chambered for a variety of 40 mm rounds, including tear gas, buckshot, incendiary and high explosives. Weighing in at twenty pounds when fully loaded, the MM-1 had an effective range of some 130 yards, but Bolan would be firing from much closer this evening, given the weather conditions.

He had no way of knowing if the cars were armored, but he went with high-explosive rounds on general principle. From two blocks out, he had the lead car in his sights, allowing it to close the gap.

It would require a swift one-two to catch them all, but even if he missed the tail car, Bolan would be satisfied. The whole point was to rattle Obregon and keep him rattled for the next few hours while his brother's life was hanging in the balance, anything to keep him from concocting a defense.

One block, and it was nearly close enough to satisfy him. The Executioner watched over open sights as the lead crew wagon rolled toward him like some kind of predatory animal in search of prey. They were a half mile from the flat where he had lifted Pablo Obregon, the police still picking through the carnage, and he calculated that the hit would go down fast enough to let him slip away before the sirens started wailing in his ear.

Unless it fell apart.

Another half block did the trick, and Bolan put his first round through the point car's grille, already shifting to his secondary target as the hood flew backward, riding on a fiery mushroom, flattening against the windshield with a crash. The car stopped short—no engine left to power it along—and smoke poured out from somewhere underneath the chassis. Doors flew open, gunners piling out in panic, and he left them to it, moving on.

The tail car's driver had already shifted to reverse, and Bolan caught him with seconds to spare, dropping his second 40 mm round directly through the rain-slick windshield. That was all it took to close the back door on the convoy, trapping the two middle cars between flaming hulks in the middle of the block. His biggest problem now would be the soldiers who were scrambling clear and looking for a target, each man brandishing a weapon as he hit the pavement running.

The warrior concentrated on the trapped cars first, unloading his third and fourth rounds in rapid fire, watching the vehicles blow apart in oily clouds of flame. The fuel tanks caught a moment later, new explosions ripping through the shattered hulks and spewing fire in all directions, streamers arcing through the night.

A couple of the gunners weren't swift enough to save themselves, flames leaping from their hair and clothing as they ran pell-mell across the battleground, screaming their lives out, burning in spite of the rain. Their comrades were disoriented, breaking right and left, still vague on where the hostile fire was coming from. Without a muzzle-flash, the MM-1 had served him well so far, and Bolan kept it busy, hesitant to set it down in favor of the M-16 A-1 that lay beside him on the ground.

He spied three gunners racing for the cover of a doorway on his left and swung the launcher back in their direction, leading them the way a hunter leads a deer. He sighted, squeezed the trigger, and the high-explosive can came down on target, detonating several feet in front of the unlucky runners, shrapnel and the shock wave blowing them away.

They might survive, but it was out of Bolan's hands. He wasn't looking for a body count so much as a reaction from the man in charge. He could have broken contact with the enemy at that point, let it go, but he wasn't inclined to let them off so easily.

These men were killers, every one of them a veteran of the drug wars terrorizing Bogotá and Medellín. Each one had bloody hands, and there was no way to tabulate their victims through the years.

And it was Judgment Day, at least for some.

Two runners raced along the sidewalk to his right, about forty yards away, and Bolan chased them with an HE round that knocked them sprawling, boneless rag-doll figures thrashing in the wind and rain. Firelight and nearby street lamps gave him the illumination he required for tracking targets, sweeping left and right to cover both sides of the street.

How many down so far? He counted seven on the deck and estimated three or four inside the tail car, probably incinerated by his second round. That left four or five to play with, but his time was running short.

As if on cue, a gunner showed himself across the street, emerging from the doorway of a camera shop and squeezing off a burst of submachine-gun fire in Bolan's general direction. It was close, at that, the bullets chipping brick and plaster several feet above his head, and the Executioner didn't wait for his opponent to correct his aim.

The shop was someone's livelihood, but he could only hope they were insured. In any case, the gunner was demanding prompt attention.

Bolan lined up his sights on the doorway, squinting in the windblown rain, and squeezed the trigger gently. With

a heavy popping sound, the high-explosive can was on it
way, descending into shadow, blossoming in flame an
thunder as the impact fuse went off.

The blast propelled the Executioner's adversary out o
hiding, right across the sidewalk to the middle of the street
The smoking corpse still bore marginal resemblance to
human being, even with the left arm missing and the leg
bent awkwardly. It lay unmoving, facedown on the pave
ment, in a spreading slick of blood.

And that was all.

If there were two or three more out there, hiding in th
shadows, they could take the message back to Obregon
Eyewitnesses were useful that way, spreading fear amon
their comrades with the story of a swift, efficient massa
cre.

Francisco would think twice before he put another arm
in the field, and when they spoke again by telephone, h
might be more receptive to negotiations.

Otherwise, his brother would be picking up the tab.

The Executioner had earned his nickname as a snipe
back in Vietnam, and he had played no part in the occa
sional atrocities that filled the media with images of Yan
kee soldiers run amok, abusing prisoners or worse. Tha
said, he knew the seamy side of war in all its variation
and he understood that it was always brutal, never pleas
ant, sometimes downright sickening.

The test of a professional was making do with what yo
had and improvising as you went along. There was a rul
that Bolan tried to follow, handling prisoners of war, bu
circumstances altered cases. Pablo Obregon was special i
his way, just like Alicia Grandier. If Bolan had to weig
one life against the other, it would be no contest. He ha
taken this assignment knowing the Colombians would hav
to die, and it made little difference to him in the long ru
how these executions were achieved.

Humanity was relative.

When blameless hostages were threatened and abuse
the Executioner would use all means at his disposal to r
lieve them from their plight. If that meant dressing Pabl

n a clown suit or reducing him to cold cuts with a rusty
utter knife, so be it. Bolan's first concern was for the in-
ocent civilians caught up in his war.

The predators could take care of themselves.

He grabbed the M-16 A-1 and faded back into shadow,
noving toward his waiting vehicle. Behind him all was
:haos, raindrops splattering and spreading gasoline with-
ut extinguishing the fire it carried, gutters lighting up,
moke hanging low across the whole block like a layer of
vil-smelling clouds.

He left the killing ground to any chance survivors and
he uniforms that would be pouring in to cordon off the
lock. The Executioner was on his way to other hunting
grounds.

And game was plentiful around Hollandia.

RAMON GUTIERREZ TOOK four soldiers with him to the
meeting, armed and brooding in the black sedan. A summons from Francisco Obregon was neither usual nor
omething to anticipate with longing. It could only mean
ad news, a fact reinforced by the very tone of his voice on
he telephone.

There was no hint of what the problem was. That would
ave been expecting too much, flying in the face of logic.
Ie would wait to drop the bomb when they were face-to-
ace.

And that was why Gutierrez had his soldiers with him.
ny larger number would have seemed belligerent instead
f merely cautious. Fewer would have been a waste. Five
uns, including Ramon's Glock 23, struck a happy me-
lium, providing a measure of security without appearing
o deliberately provoke the Colombian.

The meeting place had been Francisco's choice, a small
ark in the southeast quarter of Hollandia. The night was
vearing on, and while Gutierrez felt the past few hours had
een helpful, even pleasant, he wasn't prepared to bank on
ny guarantees.

He had a solid edge against Martin Grandier now, bu
nothing was certain in life. It could still blow up in his fac
if he let his guard down even for a moment.

Victory would only be a sure thing once the votes wer
cast and counted, placing Armand Castillo in the prim
minister's office for his first six-year term. Once that wa
accomplished, Gutierrez could begin to relax.

"They beat us here." His driver pointed through th
windshield, following the path their headlights made. Th
DGI hitter leaned forward, picking out the dark shape o
a limousine that occupied the smallish parking lot alone.

"I want some space between us," Gutierrez said.

"Right."

The rain had slacked off once again, however briefl
but the pavement glistened, and Gutierrez could hear th
foliage dripping as he stepped out of the car, his soldier
close behind him. Obregon's driver got out of the limo an
walked around to open the door for his boss, Francisc
looking stylish in his custom-tailored suit. The limo's dom
light showed an empty passenger compartment, but Gu
tierrez wasn't convinced the dealer would have come alone

"You brought some playmates," Francisco com
mented. "What's the matter? Do I scare you?"

"These are scary times. People are getting killed all ove
town."

"My people, mostly," Obregon replied. "You wouldn
know what's causing that, by any chance?"

"I lost some people, too."

"And got a new one, what I understand."

"I don't know what you mean," Gutierrez said. B
hind him he could feel his soldiers tensing, prepared fo
anything.

"I mean the woman," Obregon informed him. "What'
her-name, the old man's daughter."

"I don't—"

"Bullshit! Someone bagged her, and it wasn't me. Th
narrows down the field, if you get my drift."

"What makes you think—"

"I don't think anything, Ramon. I know the way you perate, the way your mind works. All that fucking cloak-nd-dagger business you were raised on. Now, you had a ood idea, I grant you that. I had the same idea myself and ever got a chance to pull it off. But now it's going bad, nd all the heat comes down on me. I don't like that."

"Suppose you're right," Gutierrez said. "What then? I an't just give her back like nothing happened."

"We're not communicating. You still think I'm *asking* ou to give her up. That's wrong. I'm telling you. My rother's life is on the line for what you did, and if I lose im over this, you'll wish your mother died before she ever 1et your miserable father. Am I getting through that bony Zuban skull of yours?"

Gutierrez felt the anger flaming in his cheeks. Behind im he could hear his soldiers shifting, restless, anxious to espond but still afraid of Obregon.

"You have an evil tongue, Francisco."

"And you," he said, smiling, "have something on your hirt."

Gutierrez glanced down and saw the red dot centered on is chest. He blinked and turned to check his soldiers. Each man's face or chest was similarly marked with a rimson circle—laser sights attached, no doubt, to rifles or automatic weapons, gunners hidden somewhere in the ripping darkness of the park. Ramon knew he would ever reach his Glock before the bullets cut him down. His roops were useless, neutralized.

"What is it that you want?" he asked at last.

"The woman. Is she still alive?"

Gutierrez nodded grudgingly.

"And fit to travel?"

Yet another nod.

"I will accept delivery within the hour. All arrange-1ents for her safe return will go through me. Your prob-1ms are behind you now, Ramon...unless you try to cheat 1e."

"Why would I do that?" Gutierrez asked, defeated.

"Stubborn pride, perhaps. Machismo. It would be a se rious mistake."

"Where shall I leave her?"

"Go directly home. You will receive a call in fiftee minutes. Follow your instructions to the letter, and yo won't have any difficulties."

"What about the rest of it?" he asked. "The men wh want her back?"

Francisco smiled, a grim, reptilian expression, totall devoid of warmth. "I'm taking care of them myself. Don worry. All you have to do is follow orders."

Fuming at the humiliation he was suffering in front c his men, Gutierrez nodded stiffly. "I'll be waiting for yo call."

"I knew you weren't a total fool, Ramon, no matte what the people say."

ray dawn lightened the sky outside the booth as Bolan
ropped his coins into the public telephone and dialed the
umber for Francisco's private line and waited, listening
» wind-lashed rain against the glass. A few more hours,
the weatherman was right, and they would feel the full
»rce of the storm, now dubbed Arturo.

With any luck at all, he just might beat the deadline.

Either way, though, Bolan told himself, Arturo wouldn't
e the only storm in town.

It was a different houseman this time, but he offered
othing in the way of arguments when Bolan asked for
»bregon. Another moment, and Francisco's voice came
n the line.

"I'm listening," the dealer said.

"I hope so. Have you got the woman?"

"Yes."

"She's well?"

"There was a minor problem with retrieval," Obregon
formed him, and the Executioner could feel his flesh be-
n to crawl.

"Explain."

"Whatever you may think, I didn't have her when you
lled the first time. Still, I managed to discover where she
as and get her back for you. Unfortunately she wasn't
rrounded by the gentlest, most respectable of men."

"Let's hear the damage," Bolan said. "Your brother
ill might owe me something."

"She was not dishonored, but her captors tried to question her—about her father's business, I presume. The[y]
substituted enthusiasm for imagination."

That would mean a beating at the very least. Hi[s]
knuckles whitened as he held the telephone receiver to hi[s]
ear. "I'm waiting for the bottom line."

"Some bruises," Obregon replied, "but nothing serious, in my opinion. I am not a doctor, but she walks without assistance, speaks coherently. There seem to be n[o]
broken bones. I had some food prepared, and she at[e]
well."

"I hope, for Pablo's sake, this isn't bullshit."

"I will not do anything to jeopardize my brother['s]
safety," Obregon replied.

"His life depends on you," Bolan said. "Keep that fac[t]
in mind, and you might get by."

"Of course."

Too slick, too easy, but the Executioner saw nothing t[o]
be gained by argument.

"We'll make the swap in sixty minutes. You know th[e]
botanical gardens?"

"I haven't been there," Obregon replied, "but I can fin[d]
the place."

"Do that. One hour, on the dot. You bring the woma[n,]
I'll bring Pablo. We can do some business."

"I look forward to it."

"Do I have to warn you what will happen to you[r]
brother if you're planning something tricky?"

"I believe we understand each other."

"Fair enough."

He severed the connection, standing for another mo[-]
ment in the echo chamber of the phone booth, feeling [it]
shudder with another strong gust of wind. When he coul[d]
put it off no longer, Bolan threw the sliding door back[,]
squinting as he ducked his head and dashed into th[e]
plunging wall of water, moving swiftly toward his nearb[y]
car.

Inside the rental, dripping wet, he twisted the ignitio[n]
key and steered back toward the safe house, where Enciz[o]

would be keeping Pablo company. He didn't like to leave the two of them alone too long, although he trusted Encizo to act like a professional. Their hostage was a cocky bastard, with a mouth that made you long to shut it permanently.

Soon.

Whatever else Francisco promised, Bolan had no doubt that there would be a grim surprise in store at the exchange site. Obregon couldn't allow himself to be embarrassed publicly. If he didn't retaliate for the Executioner's challenge to the family honor, he would soon be out of business, marked as easy prey for any pirate with a gun and twenty pesos' worth of nerve.

The trick, he realized, would be to lift Alicia from the trap and turn it back on Obregon. Whatever else went down that morning, he would have to try to keep the woman safe from further harm.

Bolan concentrated on his driving and the plan that he had laid to crush the Obregon brothers.

ALICIA HEARD the footsteps coming, finishing her business in the tiny bathroom and returning to her simple bed before the door swung open to admit Francisco Obregon. She recognized his face from photographs the DEA had shown her father early in the campaign, and she had seen him when she arrived at this new prison in Hollandia.

She still had no clear fix on why Ramon Gutierrez had delivered her to Obregon, but they were all the same, corrupt and violent men aligned against her father, working for Armand Castillo through election day. Beyond that point, if they succeeded, then New Amsterdam would be their playground for at least the next six years.

"I hope you're feeling better," Obregon remarked. "It's time for us to leave."

"Where are we going?" Alicia asked.

"You are going home. I'm taking care of business."

She didn't believe him. There was something in his eyes that gave the lie to soothing words. Francisco Obregon was like a vampire from the movies, she decided. Not so bad to look at when he came to you in human form, but there was boundless evil trapped behind the smiling face. He could unleash that power at will, destroy his adversaries and intimidate police, the very government designed to stop such men and punish their transgressions.

"Why?"

It was a simple question, but it made Francisco blink. He instantly recovered, and the oily smile was back in place.

"My business sometimes forces me to deal with clumsy and impulsive men," he said. "It was a serious mistake for them to interfere with you in such a way. I hope you will believe they neither had my blessing nor support."

"I don't believe you." She was angry now, refusing to be patronized as if she were an idiot.

"In any case, you will be home within the hour," Obregon went on. "Your father is expecting you. We must be going now."

Alicia still expected some cruel trick, but she appeared to have no choice. Her headache had subsided somewhat, with the food and aspirin her latest captors had provided. No one in the house had raised a hand to harm her, but she obviously couldn't trust them.

She was still a witness, still alive and fit to testify. The fact that Obregon appeared to be intent on freeing her didn't erase the past few hours by any means. She had been kidnapped by Ramon Gutierrez and his toady, Erno Soto, roughed up by Gutierrez in a crude interrogation and delivered to Francisco Obregon when she refused to answer any questions dealing with her father's campaign strategy. The link between Gutierrez and Obregon made them conspirators under the law, and she would gladly testify against both men at the first opportunity.

Plainly speaking, Obregon couldn't afford to let her live. Alicia's future testimony was a dagger pointed at his heart. It would be foolish for him to release her, and whatever else the man might be, she didn't take him for a fool.

Accepting that he meant to kill her, she had to ask herself why he intended to go through the charade of a release. It would be simple for his men to drag her out and put a bullet in her head, discard her body in the woods somewhere or bury her at sea. There had to be some reason for the game, and therein she began to glimpse a ray of hope.

The longer she survived, the greater were her chances of escape. It seemed hopeless at the moment, granted, but Alicia Grandier had never been a quitter. If nothing else, her chances might improve simply by leaving this house and the room that had become her prison cell.

She would play along and see what happened next. The worst that could happen—her own sudden death—was already a given. Each moment that prolonged her life and postponed the inevitable was a point in her favor, renewing the hope of escape.

And where was Raul Camacho now that she needed him? Where was Mike Belasko, with his talent for mayhem? Were either of them searching for her? Did they even know she had been kidnapped by their common enemy?

"All right," she said. "I'm ready."

And she would be when the time came. Alicia swore that to herself.

If this turned out to be her last day on earth, she wouldn't go meekly, quietly, into the grave. Not while she had an ounce of strength remaining.

For the first time in her adult life, she was prepared to fight.

"YOU NEED TO USE the toilet," Rafael Encizo told his captive, "now's the time."

"I'll save it," Pablo Obregon replied. "It won't be long before I'm pissing on your grave."

"Suit yourself," Encizo said. "I understand you don't mind soggy trousers in a pinch."

The dealer lost his smile at once, his features twisted in a hate-filled mask. "If you think you're so damned tough, why don't you take these handcuffs off? We'll find out who's the bigger man."

"If I take the cuffs off, Pablo, I'll have to kill you. Now, I wouldn't mind, you understand, but as it is, I need your sorry ass alive for—" Enzico stopped and checked his watch "—another fifty minutes."

"Big talk. You believe Francisco will permit this insult to go unavenged?"

"I'm counting on your brother to display his usual intelligence. Of course, if you think he'd take chances with your life, I guess you know him best."

That made the dealer hesitate, but only for a moment. He was long on confidence, this son of Medellín, long insulated from the harsh realities of gutter warfare by his brother's money and his reputation for ferocity.

"You're full of shit," Obregon said. "You want to know how many men I've killed? Just me alone?"

"I'm not your priest."

"Eighteen so far. I look at you, I see the number nineteen on your forehead. Maybe you should check the mirror."

"I'm surprised that you can count that high. Your brother let you keep the books or what? I wouldn't be surprised if you came up short from time to time."

"You saying that I'd rob my family, you piece of shit?"

"I think you'd sell your mother on the street for a handful of change, if you could remember who she was."

Pablo lurched erect, taking the straight-backed chair with him, hands securely cuffed behind his back. Enzico had no trouble dodging him, his right hand lashing out in a short jab that ended in jarring contact with the dealer's jaw. Obregon went down in a heap, and by the time he came around, he had been muzzled by a twist of silver duct tape, his wrists cuffed to a chain around his waist.

"I thought we'd try a little something different," Enzico informed him. "This is what they wear in prison when they get a little rowdy. You should get accustomed to it, just in case you manage to survive the morning."

Pablo muttered something from behind the tape, his eyes flashing hatred, but Enzico merely laughed at him and turned away. The punk was helpless now, and would be until the moment they exchanged him for Alicia Gran-dier.

From that point on, he knew, it would be anybody's game.

The Cuban spent another moment with his weapons, double-checking the Beretta and the MP-5 K submachine gun, extra magazines, the shoulder sling that fit beneath his raincoat, barely showing off a bulge. Nobody would be close enough to notice in the storm—except, perhaps, the Obregons—and they were meant to notice, understand that any hostile move meant death for Pablo on the spot.

There would be death enough to go around, Encizo re-alized, before the morning's work was done.

Whatever happened at the prisoner exchange, if he and Bolan managed to survive, then the war would still go on. They hadn't come this far and risked so much to let it drop. The final vote might still go either way, depending on a whim, but he wasn't about to leave the Obregons in a po-sition to achieve their goal of domination in New Amster-dam.

They had come close enough.

The buck stopped here.

Or, rather, it would stop at the botanical gardens in less than an hour. Alicia would be there, or so he hoped. Alive and well, if Pablo's brother could be trusted that far.

And if she wasn't, if the swap turned out to be an am-bush, Pablo Obregon would be among the first to die. Encizo knew he would enjoy the moment when he pulled the trigger, sending that one on to his reward. It might not be professional, but it was still the truth.

Sometimes it just felt good—not killing, in and of it-self, but knowing you had rid the world of a voracious predator, perhaps saving dozens or hundreds of lives in the process. Granted, there would always be another Pablo waiting in the wings to peddle narcotics, but this one—this specific savage—would be dead and gone.

It wasn't much, perhaps, in the cosmic scheme of things, but Encizo did what he could with the materials on hand.

"Let's go."

He hoisted Pablo to his feet and shoved him toward the door.

"Watch your step there," Encizo cautioned. "If you break your leg, I'll have to shoot you like the horse's ass you are."

Pablo glared and muttered curses from behind the strip of tape.

"I'd save my breath if I were you," Encizo said. "You might not have that many left."

RAMON GUTIERREZ KNEW a thing or two about revenge. He had been educated at the feet of masters, watching those who trod the corridors of power in Havana, noting how they paid each other back for this or that imagined insult. Watching power politics in action had confirmed the lessons of his youth, when he had learned to stand his ground and slug it out with bullies rather than allowing them to steal his honor.

Lessons.

Circumstances had forced Gutierrez to submit when Obregon demanded the surrender of his hostage. Worse than having laser-sighted weapons trained upon him in the darkness, he had known that any open break with Obregon would violate his orders from Havana. Men of power and influence at home were counting on their share of money from the drug trade, and Gutierrez would be held accountable if he upset the applecart.

Unless, of course, he found another enemy to take the blame.

Francisco was preparing to release the woman; that much was apparent. Half a dozen phone calls had informed the Cuban that Pablo Obregon was missing, and that more of the Medellín gunners had been killed in a series of hit-and-run attacks. The raid against Castillo headquarters that very night provided the final piece of the puzzle.

Someone was seeking the woman's release through a campaign of counterterrorism. Most of that effort was directed toward the Obregons, and it was paying off. Fran-

cisco was about to fold, give up the woman in exchange for
Pablo and a momentary respite from attack. If nothing
else, he would be buying time—unless Gutierrez took a
hand in the proceedings and derailed Francisco's effort.
That way, when it blew up in the dealer's face, his name-
less enemy—the CIA or DEA, whoever—would be blamed
for his destruction. No one in Havana would suspect Gutierrez, when he followed orders to the letter, kept his nose
clean, always did as he was told.

The raw mechanics of his plan were simple. All he had
to do was shadow Obregon until Francisco or his people
went to make the swap. Gutierrez would be on hand with
his most trusted soldiers, ready to clean house. If he could
find out who was waging war against Castillo, crush the
enemy along with Obregon, Havana might reward him for
his efforts. Who could say?

In any case, he would repay Francisco for the insults and
humiliation he had suffered. Starting now, this minute.

The surveillance had paid off in record time. Gutierrez's scouts had alerted him to movement, trailing Obregon and company when they departed from the dealer's
hideout with the woman under guard. It was a short run
to the botanical gardens, Ramon keeping in touch with his
men by cellular phone, directing them with a layout of the
killing ground in his mind's eye.

The gardens were closed at that hour, unlikely to open
at all in the face of the storm. There would be personnel on
duty—a skeleton crew to watch for damage, at the very
least—but they would be easy to deal with, no match for
Gutierrez and his troops.

Gutierrez had about two dozen men remaining in his
private army, some two-thirds of them responding to his
latest call. The others would be dealt with later, when he
had the time. For now he would be outgunned by the Obregons, and he had no idea what kind of force the name-
less enemy would field.

Surprise was everything. If he could get it right, inflict
sufficient damage in the first few seconds of the conflict,
then he would succeed. If anything went wrong, Gutierrez

knew it would be better if he went down fighting with his men. There would be no place in the world that he could hide from both the Medellín cartel and his superiors in Cuba.

Victory or death.

It was the kind of game Ramon Gutierrez understood.

The only game in town.

IT WAS A TRICKY proposition going in. He hadn't bothered telling Obregon to come alone, since it would be a waste of breath. It stood to reason that the dealer would have something up his sleeve, a plan to lift his brother, punish Bolan and eliminate Alicia all at once.

So be it.

In the circumstances, Bolan did the best he could. Encizo was his life-insurance policy, sequestered in the rain-lashed greenery ahead of schedule with his M-16 A-1/M-203, prepared to try to tip the balance when Obregon made his play. If nothing else, his presence gave the Executioner a bit more confidence.

Perhaps, with any luck at all, a winning edge.

Two men against how many?

He was counting as he drove into the parking lot, with Pablo Obregon beside him in the rental's shotgun seat, hands manacled, lips sealed with heavy duct tape. He could feel the young Colombian perk up at sight of four black limos lined up side by side, grilles pointed toward the street and Bolan's vehicle as he approached.

Four limos made it twenty men, at least, not counting drivers. If Francisco packed them in, with eight men to a car, it meant that Bolan and Encizo would be facing killer odds, sixteen to one. It wouldn't be the first time, but this was open ground, with no cover to speak of beyond his own car and the storm. It was thirty yards to the cover of the gardens, assuming he could reach the chain-link fence and scale it, make his way inside before a bullet brought him down.

That was defeatist thinking, and he caught himself before it went too far. He still had Pablo and a few surprises of his own in store for Obregon—the money belt he had secured around his captive's waist, for instance, packed with C-4 plastique instead of currency. The detonator was a radio-remote job, keyed in to the smallish plastic box on Bolan's belt. There was no way for Pablo to alert his brother while his mouth was taped.

He stopped within thirty feet of the imposing limos, set the parking brake and left the rental's engine running, with the car in gear.

As Bolan watched, the gunners unloaded from their limos, lining up like one hellacious firing squad. He counted twenty guns, the drivers still in place, before he spotted Obregon, Alicia close beside him, both already drenched with rain.

"Okay," he said to Pablo, "it's show time."

The Executioner got out on the driver's side, reached in and dragged the dealer after him. Behind his prisoner, he held a Colt Commando, an abbreviated version of the M-16 A-1, with a shorter barrel and telescoping stock, but the original's deadly firepower intact. Like Encizo's assault weapon, Bolan's also mounted a 40 mm M-203 grenade launcher under the barrel, his loaded with an antipersonnel buckshot round.

"Start walking."

He gave the younger Obregon a shove and fell in step one pace behind him, using Pablo as a human shield. Francisco's gunners had sufficient spread to nail him from the flanks, but it was close enough, considering the wind and poor visibility, for them to hesitate before they cut loose on the boss's baby brother.

"That's far enough."

They stopped twenty yards away, Bolan staring at Francisco and Alicia though the rain. The signal, if and when it came, would come from Obregon—perhaps a word or gesture, something arranged with his assassins.

"I have the woman, as you see," Francisco called across the intervening ground. "She's getting wet. Perhaps, if we make haste—"

The sound of automatic-weapons' fire exploded from the greenery behind Bolan's adversaries, bullets whispering across the rain-swept parking lot. From the expression on Francisco's face, the way he ducked to save himself and dragged Alicia after him, it was apparent that his men weren't responsible.

Who, then?

Before the Executioner could come to grips with that one, Pablo Obregon was off and running through the rain and flying bullets, racing toward the cover of his brother's line. On the firing line, approximately half of Obregon's men had reversed directions, firing toward the park.

Bolan dodged back toward his rental, reached inside and freed the parking brake. As the car rolled forward, he raised the Colt Commando to his shoulder and triggered the 40 mm buckshot round.

Whatever happened in the next few moments, it was party time. There might be only losers when the smoke cleared, but the Executioner wasn't about to die alone.

16

Encizo heard the gunners coming, settled in his sniper's nest twelve feet above the soggy ground, but he couldn't be sure whose men they were. They did their best to travel silently, assisted by the pouring rain, but most of them were city boys without a clue to stealthy woodcraft. Even with the downpour, Encizo was estimating numbers by the time they came in view, and he watched as they formed a skirmish line, guns aimed in the direction of the parking lot.

Out there the action was unfolding more or less on schedule, Obregon arriving with his limousines, and Bolan pulling in a moment later, bringing Pablo as his party favor. They were getting down to business, moving toward the swap, when someone gave a signal to the creepers in the underbrush and they cut loose with everything they had.

It went to hell from there, Encizo giving up on his attempt to figure out who stood to gain from scuttling the exchange. He had a glimpse of Pablo Obregon in flight, his brother's gunmen swinging to confront the menace on their flank, while Bolan dodged back toward his rental car.

The Phoenix Force warrior chose a target, stroked the trigger on his M-203 launcher and watched the high-explosive round explode, a giant red-orange blossom opening with sudden thunder for accompaniment, flinging bodies left and right. The sound of screams rose up to meet his ears, and there was a hesitation on the firing line as gunners glanced around and wondered what was going on.

He took advantage of their brief confusion, chambering another HE round and aiming toward the far end of the line, fifty yards distant. The launcher had no major recoil, and it was a simple thing to mark the course of his grenade, anticipating the explosion. When it came, another thunderclap with screaming echoes, he was ready for it, satisfied with the result.

And momentary satisfaction almost got Encizo killed.

He missed the gunners moving up beneath him, closing on the tree that he had chosen for his roost. They had him spotted and were raising submachine guns skyward by the time he noticed furtive movement on the ground.

It was the rain that saved Encizo, driving into his adversaries' eyes and briefly ruining their aim. They rushed it, squeezing off before they had a decent fix, and he was airborne, plummeting to earth as bullets flayed the fork where he had rested moments earlier. The gunners kept on firing up at nothing, blinded for a moment, thinking he was pinned between converging streams of fire.

And recognized their terrible mistake when Encizo rose up before them from a clump of ferns, the M-16 A-1 responding to their hostile fire with short precision bursts.

He took the left-hand gunner first because the guy was closer by a foot or two, and thus a more immediate concern. Encizo drilled a burst of 5.56 mm tumblers through his chest, still wondering who in hell the dead man represented even as the guy tumbled over backward like a broken mannequin.

His partner realized the gravity of his miscalculation then, but it was already too late to save himself. He lowered the muzzle of his submachine gun, still spewing bullets, stitching abstract patterns in the tree trunk, but he couldn't find his target fast enough to pull it off.

The M-16 A-1 spit out another burst and ripped the gunner open from his sternum to the buckle of his belt. Explosive impact punched him backward, dead before he hit the ground.

Away on Encizo's left, a battle raged in the parking lot, automatic weapons chattering, explosions going off like a

ehearsal for the crack of doom. He longed to go in search
of Bolan, help him out with Obregon, but there were more-
mmediate concerns. The gunners in the park, whomever
hey belonged to, represented a chaotic deviation from the
plans that he had made with the Executioner. If they were
llowed to dominate the battleground, it would be noth-
ng short of pure disaster for Encizo and Bolan.

And for Alicia Grandier.

He'd had one glimpse of the woman, huddled in the rain
beside Francisco Obregon, before it hit the fan. Encizo had
no way of knowing whether she was still alive, but he
couldn't allow himself to dwell on that. He would be no
use to the lady in a body bag, and there were enemies
nough to go around, without retreating to the bloody
parking lot.

He had to deal with first things first, and that meant
mopping up the park.

Encizo thumbed another HE round into the M-203's
breech and locked it down. That done, he pushed off
through the downpour. The battle had been joined, and
here was only one way to proceed: a brisk, direct assault
upon his enemies before they could demolish Bolan's plan
and ruin everything.

Head down, his weapon primed and ready, Rafael Encizo struck off through the rain in search of men to kill.

THE BUCKSHOT CHARGE from Bolan's 40 mm launcher had
been leveled at the rear end of his rental car, the lead pellets ripping through the trunk and fuel tank, laying down
a trail of gasoline that even driving rain wouldn't immediately wash away. He followed up with an incendiary
stick, white heat to spark the gasoline fumes and light a
comet's tail behind the driverless sedan.

No sooner had he put the rolling bomb in motion than
he dropped his left hand to the detonator at his waist, his
index finger seeking out the button, bearing down. He
glimpsed Pablo Obregon in flight, head down and shoulders hunched to duck incoming fire, before the plastique
charge around his waist went off.

And that was all for Pablo. In a heartbeat he was va
porized, a fiery mushroom rising on the spot where he ha
been. The shock wave of the blast rolled out in front of th
Colombian, rocking the nearest limousine and topplin
several of Francisco's gunners to the ground. They scram
bled back in seconds flat, but they were shaken, scorched
disoriented.

The rental car was bearing down on them, taking hit
from several weapons, bright flames rolling up its back
enveloping the trunk. It was traveling three or four mile
per hour, tops—no major threat to any of the limos from
a serious collision—but the tank had only seconds left be
fore it blew.

He thought about Alicia, somewhere close at hand, bu
there was no way he could reach her at the moment. Bo
lan fired a short burst from the hip and saw one of Fran
cisco's gunners kiss the pavement, thrashing like
grounded fish before his life ran out through half a doze
bullet holes.

Explosions rang out in the park, and that could only b
Encizo jumping in behind the ambush party, trying to dis
tract them. He was on his own in that regard, and that wa
where the best-laid plans began to fall apart. As Bola
couldn't help his Phoenix Force comrade, so Encizo wa
no help to the Executioner when it came to stopping Ob
regon.

Bolan hit the pavement on his belly, lying prone an
waiting for the rental car to reach its destination, trackin
with the Colt Commando as the flaming hulk rolled on. I
struck the second limo from the left, colliding nose t
nose, and Bolan watched two gunners hose the rental wit
submachine-gun fire, their bullets wasted on an empty ve
hicle.

The fuel tank detonated with a roar that shook th
ground beneath him, spewing tentacles of flaming gaso
line in all directions. Bolan saw the limo's driver scrambl
clear and shot him in the chest before he had a chance t
look for cover.

Francisco's troops were starting to recover from the first shock of the ambush, using their vehicles for cover and returning fire in both directions, some firing toward the park, while others tried to get a fix on Bolan through the smoke and leaping flames.

He kept his place as searching rounds began to ricochet off pavement to his left and right, still far enough off target that the Executioner felt relatively safe. It wouldn't take his adversaries long to find the range, of course. There was no time to waste.

He thumbed a high-explosive round into the chamber of his M-203 launcher, closed the breech and sighted quickly down the barrel of his M-16 A-1. The nearest limo made a handy target, even if the bodywork was armored to deflect incoming fire. He needed a diversion, something to distract Francisco's gunners while he found a more secure position, closed the gap and put his enemies on a defensive footing.

Bolan stroked the M-203's trigger and watched the HE round impacted an inch or two above the nearest limo's grille. The hood sprang open with a clap of smoky thunder, peeling backward like the lid of a cheap aluminum can, flames licking at the engine underneath. Smoke billowed from the wounded tank, merging quickly with the greasy cloud from Bolan's sedan to briefly screen his movements.

He was up and running in a heartbeat, veering to his right around the burning limousine and closing in to meet his enemies. They would be more accustomed, he imagined, to the kind of targets that attempt to run away.

A little change of pace, then, for the soldiers of Francisco Obregon.

With any luck at all, it just might do the trick.

ALICIA GRANDIER WAS startled when the shooting started behind her. She had felt her spirits leap at the sight of Mike Belasko standing in the rain, prepared to take her home. While she didn't recognize the small man at his side, trussed up in tape and handcuffs, it was no great leap to

understand that she was part of what the military some
times called a prisoner exchange.

At the moment she was not inclined to question any
methods that resulted in her freedom. She could agonize
about morality some other time. Right now the only thing
that mattered was survival—and for all the sudden rush of
hope she felt, Alicia knew that that was still in doubt.

There were so many men and weapons ranged against
Belasko that it seemed impossible for them to simply drive
away unscathed. In that case, there would be two witnesses against her kidnappers, a situation that defied all
logic, even from her own perspective.

She was ready for a trick, then, nearly anything at
all...except what happened next. Belasko and his adversary, Obregon, were just about to make the trade when
someone opened fire behind her, from the park. The
strange part was, the unseen gunmen had been firing at her
captors rather than Belasko, pouring bullets toward the
men and limousines.

It fell apart from there, Francisco dragging her back
under cover, crouched between two cars. His men were
firing toward the park, a few of them unloading on Belasko, but she couldn't see if he was safe or whether they
had cut him down.

Alicia glimpsed a running man—Belasko's prisoner, an
awkward sprinter with his hands cuffed to a chain around
his waist—and she was watching when he suddenly exploded like a human bomb, the ghastly sight enough to
stun her.

Beside her, Obregon was cursing bitterly and shouting
at his men in Spanish. She suspected he was weeping, but
she couldn't say for sure if she was seeing tears or simply
raindrops on his face. Whatever, he was raging at his men
to kill Belasko, and then there was another, still more
powerful explosion, flaming gasoline falling from the sky
like superheated rain and pooling underneath the limo on
her left.

Francisco had a pistol in his hand. He grabbed her arm
and dragged her toward the rear of the limo, moving in an

awkward crouch. Above her head a bullet struck the fender of the limousine with a resounding crack and fell, deformed and flattened, at Alicia's feet.

She felt exposed and vulnerable even crouched between the cars. She didn't understand the physics of a ricochet precisely, but she knew they weren't safe, despite the walls of Detroit steel on either side of them. Her captor obviously knew it, too, for he was cursing, bobbing up to check the parking lot, the wall of trees and bushes on the other side.

It struck Alicia that the gunfire from the park was slacking off a bit, though she could still hear shots and the occasional explosion emanating from that source. In fact, as she considered it, it seemed more accurate to say a portion of the fire was now directed elsewhere, granting Obregon and his remaining men a measure of relief.

"We're going!" Francisco snapped, dragging her behind him as he duck walked toward the rear end of the limousine.

"But where?"

"Shut up and come with me!"

She had no choice, in fact, as Obregon pulled her closer, shoving the snout of his pistol against her ribs. Alicia's hair was plastered to her skull by now, her clothes soaked through, but it wasn't a cold rain, thankfully. She felt as if she had been standing in the shower with her clothes on, and it would have been enough to make her laugh out loud, except that she was terrified of being shot at any moment.

"This way!"

Obregon was on his feet now, crowding her in front of him, jogging toward the park at an oblique angle. Bullets whispered past them, somewhere on Alicia's right, but it didn't appear that anyone was seriously trying to stop them. Ahead of her she saw another fireball blossom in the man-made forest, screams erupting in its wake.

What was it? What was happening?

"Come on, goddammit!" Obregon shoved harder now, the pistol jabbing at Alicia's spine. She almost lost her footing on the rain-slick pavement, but Francisco held her upright and propelled her toward the looming shadows of the park.

They reached a turnstile with an empty ticket booth beside it, and she scrambled over, with Francisco close behind her, clinging to a fistful of her soggy blouse. Alicia felt the buttons pop, but gave no thought to modesty. It was her chance, perhaps the only one that she would have.

She ducked and twisted, left the blouse behind her like a reptile sloughing off its skin. Once more she almost lost her balance, sliding in a puddle, but she managed to remain upright by virtue of her desperation, sprinting for the cover of the nearby trees.

Francisco overtook her before she knew that he was even gaining. Her first warning was the impact of his fist between her shoulder blades, then she went down on all fours.

"Bitch!" He sounded breathless, furious. "Try that again, and you won't have to think about the others, do you hear me? I'll kill you myself."

Alicia was hoisted to her feet, her left arm twisted up behind her back. Obregon shoved her in front of him, into the trees.

Her chance was gone, the moment wasted. There was nothing she could do to save herself from this point on.

But she wouldn't give up without a fight, Alicia vowed. If she was doomed, at least she could resist her would-be killer, make things difficult for him along the way.

Closing her mind to the pain from her hands, knees and shoulder, she waited, looking forward to the time when she could turn and strike.

RAMON GUTIERREZ HUNKERED in the rain, an Uzi submachine gun in his hands, and tried to figure out exactly how and when the ambush had begun to fall apart.

The plan was flawless in conception, and he knew his men hadn't been spotted entering the park. His targets—Obregon and company, the woman and a stranger covering Francisco's brother—seemed oblivious to their approaching doom. It all seemed perfect, up until the very moment when his soldiers opened fire across the parking lot.

And then it all blew up in his face.

Gutierrez still had no clear fix on who was firing at his men or why. At first he thought Francisco might have stationed spotters in the garden, but if so, they should have opened up the moment that Ramon's commandos showed themselves, before they had an opportunity to fire on the Colombians.

And yet, who else?

He ducked his head and cursed as a grenade went off ten or fifteen yards in front of him. None of his people were armed with grenades, so where in the hell were they coming from?

His index finger tightened on the Uzi's trigger, nearly squeezing off an aimless burst into the shrubbery. He caught himself before he wasted precious ammunition and betrayed his hiding place to the unseen, faceless enemy.

He didn't even know the number of his adversaries yet, but several of his own men had been killed or wounded. That was clear enough from the agonized screams that followed each explosion, the severed arm that he had nearly tripped on as he scuttled through the undergrowth.

It was apparent to Gutierrez that Armand Castillo's dreams were going down the toilet. One way or another, something had gone wrong. He still couldn't make up his mind if he should blame the CIA or someone from Colombia, an enemy the Obregons had underestimated in their reckoning, but it made little difference either way. The jig was up, as Yankee capitalists liked to say, and all Ramon could think of at the moment was his own escape.

Havana sounded better all the time.

Gutierrez shifted to his left, moving slowly and cautiously back the way he had come when he entered the park. It would take him longer, moving in a huddled crouch, and while he feared the arrival of the police, Ramon was more afraid of being cut down by a sniper's bullet or the shrapnel from an exploding hand grenade.

Arrest was one thing; he could always post the bond, skip out before his trial. But death was permanent, with no appeals and no reprieve.

As if in answer to his thoughts, a burst of gunfire cut through the foliage overhead, missing Gutierrez by inches. He flattened himself on the mossy earth, twisting his head to one side when he landed facedown in a puddle of standing rainwater. It would be the crowning insult, he decided, if he drowned while hiding from a gunman that he couldn't even see.

Gutierrez started to creep on his belly, worming through the ferns and grass until he reached a man-made path, complete with pebbled stepping-stones. Hesitant, almost afraid to move, he poked his head out and glanced both ways along the path before he rose to his hands and knees. When no one shot him down, Gutierrez took a chance and scrambled to an awkward crouch, the Uzi clutched against his chest.

The path would be his best hope for a swift retreat, he realized. It led back toward the section of the park where he had entered with his men a lifetime earlier. Of course, the risks were greater, too. It meant that he would have to travel in the open, visible to any snipers in the area. An easy shot.

Another burst of automatic fire behind him helped decide the issue. Gutierrez burst from cover with a muffled curse, sprinting along the path with rain slashing into his face, forcing his eyes into slits. He had covered all of twenty yards when it happened, the earth rearing up in front of him, smoke and dust in his face, the sound of roaring thunder in his ears.

Already airborne, sailing backward through a looping somersault, he had a fair idea of what had happened—a grenade on the path.

The ground rushed up to meet him like a giant fist, and darkness swallowed him alive.

17

Bolan came around the limo at a dead run, firing from the hip. His initial burst caught a startled gunner in his chest and slammed him back against the car, legs folding as he slithered to the pavement, dead eyes open to the pouring rain.

Beyond the body of his first kill, Bolan met two more of Obregon's commandos. Both men were armed with submachine guns, seeking target acquisition as the Executioner burst into view, the Colt Commando stuttering.

On the warrior's left, the taller of the two men started twitching through a jerky little dance step, screaming as the 5.56 mm bullets ripped his shirt and jacket into tatters. Staggering, he dropped the muzzle of his subgun but held the trigger down, a spray of parabellum manglers shearing off one kneecap, riddling both his feet before he fell.

The second gunner was more agile on his feet, despite an extra forty pounds around his waist. He sidestepped, squeezing off a short burst from his MP-5 SD-3 with the custom silencer attached, a sound like ripping canvas emanating from the muzzle as his rounds went high and wide.

The Colt Commando stitched holes across the shooter's chest before he could correct his faulty aim. The impact spun him like a dervish, firing as he made a full three-sixty, spent brass leaping from the subgun's ejection port. The magazine was empty by the time he wobbled back to face the Executioner, and there was no fight left in him by then, a dead man standing upright in the heartbeat it required for gravity to pull him down.

Bolan pressed on, leaping over the corpse without a break in stride, sweeping the scene for some glimpse of Alicia or Francisco Obregon. Neither was visible as the warrior reached the second limousine in line and crouched behind it, feeling the heat of spreading flames on his face. How long before the limo's gas tank blew? Or would the rain prevent that happening?

No matter.

He could hear the numbers counting down in his head, and there were still more gunners to be dealt with. If nothing else, the wild fire from the park had slackened off, and he gave Encizo the credit there. It was unfortunate that the Phoenix Force warrior had been kept from joining Bolan in his battle for the parking lot, but Encizo had paid his way and then some by disrupting the ambush... whomever it belonged to.

Bolan fed the M-203 with another buckshot round, afraid to use HE at such close quarters, when Alicia might be huddled trapped within the killing radius. Emerging from his cover, the warrior found three gunners lined up to receive him, glaring over automatic weapons and the corpses of their comrades.

The M-203 belched its load of double-aught projectiles, fifty pellets bursting from the muzzle of what amounted to a giant sawed-off shotgun. At a range of fifteen feet, the blast was devastating, with the middle gunner talking most of it, his face a blur as impact knocked him back and out of play.

And that left two.

Both men were wounded, one with his left arm and side in bloody tatters, while his comrade had been stricken in the leg, dumped on his backside in the rain. The two gunners still had weapons in their hands, however, and the Executioner would have to finish them before he went in search of other prey.

The Colt Commando spit out two staccato bursts, roughly five or six rounds each, and it was done. The gunner with the shredded arm jerked violently, as if a live electric wire had landed in the puddle at his feet, and went down on his back. The seated hardman was about to call for help, when Bolan shot him in the mouth and took the best part of his head off, brushing past him on his way to other targets before the lifeless figure toppled over on its side.

The Executioner moved at will among the dead and dying now, reloading on the move, confronting danger as it came and blasting it aside. A number of Francisco's men had fallen to the ambush, lying dead or wounded on the asphalt at his feet. The rest were fighting for their lives without a clue to what was happening around them, baffled by the way in which their boss's master plan had suddenly unraveled.

It was Armageddon for the men of Medellín.

But there was no sign of Alicia Grandier, no trace of Obregon around the limos. Even peering underneath the cars, in search of stragglers, Bolan came up empty. He was rising from a crouch and feeding the Commando with another magazine when something at the corner of his eye demanded his attention.

Turning toward the park, he glimpsed Francisco and the woman disappearing in among the trees. They had eluded him somehow, and now he had to seek them in the manmade forest.

Bolan didn't hesitate.

The war was still in progress ahead of him, but it was fading by degrees. Encizo either had the situation covered, or the late arrivals had begun to turn on one another, adding further chaos to the scene.

Whatever, the Executioner had a job to do, and he wouldn't allow his quarry to escape, much less with a civilian hostage. This was all about Alicia, and losing her when he had come this far would be a travesty.

Bolan sprinted in the direction of the turnstile that would admit him to the park. Whatever lay beyond that gate, the one thing he was certain of was death.

ENCIZO GLIMPSED Ramon Gutierrez as he reached the garden path and made his break for freedom, racing down the narrow avenue between the ranks of overhanging trees. It was a tricky shot from where the Phoenix Force warrior stood, but he could trust the M-203 launcher to perform upon demand.

He led the running target, stroked the launcher's trigger and dispatched a high-explosive round to close the gap. It burst a moment later, several yards in front of the runner, and the shock wave slammed Gutierrez onto his back.

It might have been a kill, but you could never tell when HE rounds exploded in an open space. The blast went up and out primarily, and shrapnel from the casing might be vaporized on detonation. Strictly speaking, it wasn't an antipersonnel round, and Encizo knew that he would have to verify the hit to satisfy himself.

He was about to do just that when interlocking fire from several submachine guns suddenly converged on his position, pinning Encizo behind a tree. He tried to count the hostile weapons, made it three and knew that it would only be a moment now before the gunners started closing in to finish him. It was a relatively simple strategy, two soldiers firing while a third advanced, then taking turns until they had him boxed and one or more were close enough to guarantee a kill.

Assuming he allowed them to proceed.

It would be tricky, but Encizo thought that he could pull it off.

He fed the M-203 launcher with another HE round, acutely conscious of the fact that every moment wasted here allowed Gutierrez to regain his senses if the man was still alive. A full load in the M-16 A-1, and he was ready.

He had the gunners marked, at least approximately, by the sound and muzzle-flashes of their weapons. Bursting out of cover in a fighting crouch, Encizo broke to the left of the tree that had sheltered him, making target acquisition on the nearest of the shooters, roughly thirty yards away. The tree protected him from Number Two, while Number Three was on his flank, forty yards distant and closing.

He triggered the launcher, sending the 40 mm HE round to do its work, already pivoting to deal with Number Three before the deadly egg exploded in a flash of smoky thunder. Strangled screams erupted from that direction, and he had the moving gunner covered in a heartbeat, sighting down the barrel of his rifle and squeezing off a burst of 5.56 mm tumblers that ripped through palmettos and tall, lacy ferns, seeking flesh.

And found it, as his target toppled to the ground, using up the last part of his submachine gun's magazine to spray the storm clouds overhead.

Encizo circled through the greenery, a gliding shadow now, whatever sounds he made covered by the driving rain. He knew approximately where his enemy was stationed, but the gunner could have moved by now. Instead of homing on the spot directly, the Phoenix Force warrior stood still and waited, listening. He was rewarded moments later by the sound of someone charging through the undergrowth.

The shooter burst upon him, absolutely unprepared to meet his quarry in the smallish clearing, staring over gunsights. He was frozen for an instant, fumbling with his subgun. That was all it took for Encizo to end the game. A short burst from his M-16 A-1 and it was over, one more lifeless scarecrow stretched out at his feet.

That left Gutierrez, and Encizo wasted no time homing on the trail. He cursed at finding that his quarry was gone, but there were blood spots on the pebbled stepping-stones, a trail that led in the direction Gutierrez had been traveling before the HE round had stopped him in his tracks.

Encizo followed, overtook his prey short moments later, less than halfway to the fence the man had scaled to make his way inside the park. From twenty yards away, he spoke one word.

"Gutierrez."

Slowly, painfully, the DGI enforcer turned to face him. He was carrying an Uzi, but it dangled at his side. A gash along his hairline had smeared his face with blood, and from the looks of him, there were other wounds on the hardman's chest and arms, dark crimson seeping through his rain-soaked clothing.

"You."

It was a statement and an accusation all at once. Encizo recognized his adversary's hatred.

"Yes, Ramon, me."

"You ruined everything."

"I did my best."

Encizo saw the Uzi coming up, but there was no real strength or will behind it, no real challenge as he squeezed the trigger of his automatic rifle. Gutierrez dropped to the path with bullets in his chest and stomach.

Done.

A mercy round to finish it, perhaps, and speed Gutierrez on his way?

Encizo spit into the gravel of the path and started to retrace his steps. There were more-pressing matters on his mind.

Ramon could take care of himself.

"KEEP MOVING!"

With an angry shove, Francisco Obregon propelled his hostage through a waist-high wall of ferns, following on her heels and keeping her covered with his pistol. Automatic weapons rattled in the garden to his right, perhaps a hundred yards away, but they were slightly muffled by the distance, trailing off as fewer guns responded on each round of firing.

Running made Francisco feel ashamed, but he could live with it. Survival was the main thing, followed closely by revenge, and dead men had no chance at all of getting even with their enemies.

He had been watching when his brother died. A flash, a thunderclap, and Pablo was no more. For all intents and purposes, he simply disappeared.

It had been some kind of booby trap, Francisco realized. The bastards never had intended to release his brother, any more than he had meant to liberate the woman. They were taking out insurance, maybe hoping

Pablo would embrace his brother when they took the chains off, let the bomb kill two Obregons for the price of one.

Well, they had missed on that score. He was still alive, still dangerous, no matter what befell his fighters in the parking lot. Francisco had more gunmen in Hollandia, an army waiting for him back in Medellín, prepared to do his bidding.

Someone—the American, for starters—had made a very serious mistake.

The woman was about to pull ahead of him. Francisco grabbed her by the hair and dragged her back, smiling at her gasp of pain. She looked vulnerable in her bra and skirt, barefoot, her legs nicked and bleeding from a close encounter with a thornbush some yards back. He wished that there was time to punish her appropriately for her role in the destruction of his brother, but Obregon was in a hurry now. When they were clear and he had found a vehicle, he would dispatch her with a bullet to the head, let her father's grief be his reward.

The rest would follow in due time, but first he had to make his getaway. If he was killed or captured here, it meant a victory for his opponents, whoever they were.

Americans. That much was clear from Obregon's glimpse of the man who had abducted Pablo. Someone in the States was challenging his power on New Amsterdam. And if they beat him there, what then? Incursions into Medellín itself?

"Stop here!" he snapped, and held Alicia by one arm, twisting the snout of his automatic into her ribs for emphasis.

"Why?"

"Be quiet, bitch!"

He listened for the sounds of combat, hearing only silence—no gunfire from the parking lot, and no more from the trees to his right. Could it be finished? Was there any chance his soldiers had prevailed?

If so, Francisco knew they would be waiting for him at his latest safe house. And if none came back, then he would have his answer. Either way, he had to look out for himself right now.

In front of them, a narrow path wound through the garden, running east to west. Francisco didn't have a clue where it would lead, but he had a brooding fear of getting lost among the trees and wandering around in circles while his enemies were stalking him, perhaps still stranded there when the police arrived. At least, he thought, the path would take him somewhere. If it felt like danger up ahead, he could reverse directions, try the other course.

"Go left," he told Alicia, pushing her in the direction of the westbound track. She did as she was told, a frail, bedraggled figure in the pouring rain.

The bullet came from nowhere, clipped his shoulder from behind and slammed him forward so that he collided with Alicia and they both went down. The pebbled stones and gravel of the path were harsh against his knees, Francisco understanding with a portion of his mind that he had torn his slacks.

His strong right hand still clenched the automatic pistol, covering Alicia as he groveled in the path and he recovered his balance by degrees. It would have been the time to finish him but someone missed his chance, as Obregon grabbed the woman, grunting with exertion, and rolled her over on top of him.

Alicia tried to wriggle free but a light tap with his pistol on her skull was enough to settle her. That done, Francisco wormed his way into a seated posture, scooting back until his spine was pressed against a sturdy tree trunk.

"If you try to run," he whispered in Alicia's ear, "I'll kill you."

Slowly, awkwardly, he struggled to his feet and brought the woman with him, clasped before him as a living shield. It was the best that he could do.

"All right," he shouted, facing the shadows that surrounded him. "If you want this bitch, then show yourself!"

IT HADN'T BEEN a killing shot, and Bolan cursed himself for squeezing off too quickly, worrying too much about Alicia and the risk to her if his first bullet drilled completely through Obregon. Now he was dealing with a wounded predator, Alicia standing in the line of fire, his options gravely limited.

"I'm waiting," Obregon informed him. "Shall I kill her now or count to three?"

The Executioner was busy calculating odds and angles, thumbing another high-explosive round into his M-203 launcher, leaving the Colt Commando's fire-selector switch set on semiautomatic. No matter how he played it, this was going to be close.

"One!"

The dealer's voice was strained and Bolan thought Francisco might be slipping into shock. The down side was that he might panic, put a bullet in Alicia's brain if he felt consciousness begin to fade.

"Two!"

"Right here," Bolan said as he stepped onto the path. He held his weapon braced against his hip, the double muzzles angled toward a point fifteen feet above Francisco's head.

"So there you are. The man who tries to kill me, yes?"

"It crossed my mind."

"Who are you?"

"Just a sanitary engineer." He saw confusion on the dealer's face, a failure to communicate. "I take the garbage out."

"You killed my brother."

"It's a start."

"I think for you it is the end."

"Not quite."

"You want the woman, yes? I ought to kill her now, before your eyes, as punishment for Pablo, but perhaps we still can make a deal."

"I'm listening."

A lie. He heard Francisco's words, but he was really counting down the doomsday numbers, waiting for the proper moment, knowing he would feel it when it came.

"You let me walk away, don't follow me, and I will leave her for you somewhere in the city."

"Oh?"

"You don't believe me?"

"Let's just say I'm skeptical."

"What choice do you have?"

"Well, I could always blow your head off."

"Not with that," Francisco told him, nodding at the weapon Bolan carried. "You would surely kill the woman first."

Alicia's face was frozen in a mask of grim determination. Bolan read the message in her eyes, a willingness to sacrifice herself if it would make the crucial difference, but it hadn't come to that. Not yet.

"You may be right," he said to the Colombian, "and, then again—"

His index finger tightened on the trigger of the launcher, and the weapon belched its single, deadly word. He couldn't literally see the HE round in flight, but he was staring at the chosen point of impact when it detonated, shattering the tree trunk fifteen feet above Francisco's head.

The rest was chaos, flying shards of wood and leafy branches tumbling to the ground. Alicia and her captor fell before the shock wave, Obregon atop the woman for an instant, rolling clear before the worst of the debris crashed down around him.

He was lurching to his feet when Bolan found his target, squeezing off three rounds from the assault rifle in rapid fire. Francisco staggered, went down on one knee and half turned toward the woman, trying desperately to raise his automatic.

Bolan's fourth round struck the dealer underneath one eye and snapped his head back, flecks of gray and crimson spattered on the trunk behind him. Obregon was dead before he toppled over backward, and his pistol slipped from lifeless fingers as he fell.

It took another moment, dragging twisted branches off Alicia Grandier, but then he had the woman on her feet. She wore a dazed expression, dirt and ruined makeup smudged across her face, but she was breathing, standing on her own. Alive.

"You came for me," she said. And then, "Raul?"

"I'm here," Encizo told her, stepping from the undergrowth a few yards back. "Gutierrez slowed me down."

Alicia ran to meet him, stepping into the circle of the Phoenix Force warrior's arms.

"It all works out," Bolan said, picking up the first faint sound of sirens in the distance, squad cars, fire trucks, ambulances racing toward the killing ground. "We're out of time."

When they had cleared the exit, moving swiftly toward Encizo's rental car, the Cuban asked him, "What about Castillo?"

"Up and coming," Bolan replied. He glanced at Alicia, thinking of her father, waiting for her. "Let's take care of first things first."

18

Cuba

The storm had bypassed Cuba, and Armand Castillo counted himself fortunate to be home again, more or less. The small estate outside of Manzanillo wasn't truly home, of course, but it would do for now.

All things considered, Castillo knew that he was lucky not to be in prison or a shallow grave.

It had been touch and go for several days, when he returned to Cuba from New Amsterdam. His disappearance, in the wake of so much violence, had confused the media enough to let his masters off the hook. There had been speculation on a Cuban link, but he had used a phony passport and disguise when he departed from the island.

It was a mystery, and so it would remain.

His masters had been furious, of course, not only with the loss of the election, but the ruin of their partnership with Medellín. He had been questioned closely, finally persuading them that he had no idea who was responsible for killing off the Obregon brothers. There would be other opportunities to deal with the Colombians, perhaps, but Castillo for one was happy to be out of the loop.

He was happy to be alive.

Of course, he recognized that his career advancement with the DGI was finished, at least for the foreseeable future. A failure of this momentum would mark him for years to come, perhaps forever. Still, he had squeaked through the hasty court-martial without formal charges being sustained, and they would find a desk job for him somewhere in the provinces when it was safe for him to show his face.

So far, Castillo had no clear idea of how long they expected him to hide. He was in exile, under heavy guard, but not a prisoner per se. His masters in Havana were afraid he would be spotted, recognized somehow, thus revealing the link between Fidel and what had lately happened on New Amsterdam. That kind of bad publicity could bring reprisals from the Americans, even UN sanctions, if the charges could be proved.

In fact, Castillo didn't mind his hideaway. He liked the Cuban countryside, and if he seldom got to leave the grounds, at least the small estate had room enough for him to walk and exercise, a library with books enough to keep him occupied. A bit more time, and he was certain he could talk his keepers into bringing him a woman now and then.

All the comforts of home.

If there was any downside, it was simply knowing he had failed. The world—or part of it, at least—had been within his grasp, and he had fumbled, let it slip right through his fingers.

How much of the guilt lay with Ramon Gutierrez? On returning to Havana, Castillo had offered the story received from his DGI contact in Hollandia, only to learn that there was no such man on the payroll. Or so they told him anyway. Aware that he might never know the truth, Castillo still found it convenient to blame Gutierrez for much of his present disgrace.

The man was dead, and that was something to be glad about, at least. Castillo would have liked to do the job himself, but someone else had beaten him to it. There were more questions about that, what Ramon had been doing at the botanical gardens, involved in an apparent firefight with the Obregons, but Castillo was clueless, finally convincing the interrogators of his ignorance.

From the window of his study, he could see a couple of the guards outside, young men in olive-drab fatigues, with AKS-74 assault rifles slung over their shoulders. He wondered idly how many of them had ever fired their weapons anyplace beside the practice range, but it was unimportant.

How could anybody find him here?

BOLAN AND ENCIZO ENTERED Cuba through the gateway of Guantánamo, the military base occupied by American troops since the turn of the century. From there it was a relatively simple task to slip away in civvies, with Encizo serving as guide, making their way through the Sierra Maestra toward Manzanillo and their target.

Tracking Castillo had been no challenge for Aaron Kurtzman at Stony Man Farm. The trick was knowing of his DGI connection in advance, assuming that Castillo would return to Cuba in his haste to flee New Amsterdam. From there it was a straightforward matter of coordinating with the CIA and tapping an informant in the DGI itself, retrieving details of the erstwhile candidate's court-martial, the order that had sent him into "temporary" hiding at a safe house in the sticks.

The hard part would be getting inside, past Castillo's guards, to make the tag.

There had been several days of argument in Washington as to whether it was even worth the risk. Since Cuba's plan—and Medellín's—had been aborted in Hollandia, some men of influence considered reaching out to touch Castillo an extravagance, a waste of time and energy. It was decided finally—by "someone in authority," Brognola's phrase—that taking out the one-time candidate would pose an object lesson for Havana, something for Fidel and company to ponder in the days ahead if they got restless and began to think of branching out through terrorism and intrigue.

As for the Medellín cartel, new leadership had already replaced the Obregons. It would be business as usual within a matter of days, but without the Cuban connection—at least for a while.

The DEA already had its eye on Haiti, where a ranking member of the Port-au-Prince police department was suspected of distributing drug-related payoff to the tune of one hundred million dollars per year.

The more things changed, the more they stayed the same.

Bolan tried to put the recent past behind him, concentrating on his mission as they traveled through the mountains. He was content to let Encizo do the talking when they met any locals, trusting in silence and the peasant's natural reticence with strangers to get him by. The very fact that they possessed a car gave villagers good cause to think that they were party members on official business, and they managed to avoid legitimate patrols, though it was close a time or two.

The safe house was in fact a thirty-acre plot of ground, surrounded by adobe walls, the acreage thick with trees except for just around the house. Considering the Cuban mind-set and economy, it was a safe bet that there would be no elaborate security devices. But the CIA's informant had advised them that the target would be under guard around the clock.

So much for a simplistic touch and go.

It meant that they would have to take the sentries, too, and thereby multiply their risk. A fact of life in Bolan's everlasting war.

They had prepared a scale map of the hideout that was based on satellite surveillance photographs. The photos were detailed enough to let Bolan guess at the floor plan of the house, allowing for surprises once he got inside. The rest of it was stealth and legwork, pinning down the guards as quietly as possible before they went in for Castillo.

Easy, right. Like falling off a log—into an open grave.

Their weapons had been selected with anonymity in mind, nothing traceable to the United States if anything went wrong. Their main weapons were 9 mm Heckler &

Koch MP-5 SD-3 submachine guns, with factory-installed silencers and collapsing metal stocks. They backed up the stutterguns with matching Walther P-88 double-action autoloaders, their muzzles threaded to accommodate suppressors if required. Swiss cutlery and fragmentation grenades of Russian manufacture completed the deadly ensemble, guaranteed to confuse any Monday-morning quarterbacks who might come nosing through the rubble. Nothing could be left behind that pointed to U.S. involvement in the hit.

There were no dogs, no cameras or sentries on the outer wall. A moment's effort saw the Stony Man warriors crouched inside and ready to proceed. They had agreed beforehand on divergent angles of attack.

"Let's get it right this time," Encizo whispered. And with that, he vanished, gliding through the trees in the direction of the house.

"Let's get it right," the Executioner repeated, and set off toward the killing ground.

THE GUARDS WERE YOUNG and somewhat overconfident. It never really crossed their minds that there was any danger here in Mother Cuba. Their "guest" was DGI, but he was also in disfavor, someone to avoid, perhaps, but not a man to fear.

Not yet.

Their mission was routine and not a little boring. If they let their guard down now and then, who was there to complain or even care?

Encizo took the first guard with his knife, crept up behind him while the guy smoked a cigarette, and slit his throat from ear to ear. Another moment to conceal the body, more or less, and he moved on.

The next two were a team, and since he couldn't separate them, he took both of them together, coming from their blind side with the silenced Walther. One round each at point-blank range, and they were facedown on the grass. No muss, no fuss.

Again he dragged the bodies out of sight, helping him-
lf to one of the Russian-made assault rifles and a ban-
olier of extra magazines. The Phoenix Force warrior
new that silence was imperative, but if the probe began
» fall apart, it would be comforting to have some extra
repower available.

Just in case.

Number Four was another loner. He had propped his
alashnikov rifle against a tree while he relieved himself,
aguely aware of a presence behind him as Encizo stepped
orward, looped an arm beneath his chin and snapped the
ntry's neck with one sharp twist.

The house was visible from where he stood now, with the
ntry stretched out lifeless at his feet. So close and yet so
r away.

He checked his wristwatch and saw that it was time to
ove. Another pair of sentries occupied the front porch,
laxing in their matching wicker chairs. They were in
nge if he used the Kalashnikov, but that meant noise. To
g them with the subgun, he had to get in closer, find a
ay to cross the open lawn without alerting his potential
rgets.

Try a different angle. Put a corner of the house be-
veen himself and the remaining sentries. He would have
» pray that no one glanced out through a window as he
ade his move, or else that they mistook his camouflage
.tigues for a variation of the daily uniform.

Not likely, that.

These troops were green, but they were far from stupid.
nothing else, the war paint on his face and hands would
ve the game away to anyone who wasn't blind.

It all came down to speed and stealth, then, with a
odicum of pure, dumb luck.

Encizo chose his moment, crossed himself and started
gging toward the house.

RMAND CASTILLO was considering his second whiskey of
e day, unable to think of a reason why not, when sud-

denly all hell broke loose a few yards from his study. A
automatic rifle opened fire without warning, the unmis
takable sound of a Kalashnikov, and he flinched from th
sound, dropping his empty glass to the floor at his feet.

He heard another burst, that one shorter than the firs
and thought the sound was coming from the front porc
of the house. A sudden knot of panic in Castillo's gt
brought sour bile into his throat and put a grimace on h'
face.

He kept a pistol in the study, smuggled in his luggag
from Havana, as a hedge against potential treachery. I
seemed unlikely that his guards would turn against him
but he took no chances. Having seen his whole life chang
and virtually fall apart within the past few days, Castill
knew that nothing was beyond the realm of possibility.

The pistol was a 9 mm Browning BDM, the double
action model, with the removable blade sight in front an
the snag-proof adjustable rear. He drew the slide back hal
an inch to verify he had a live round in the chamber, bt
he left the hammer down to hedge against a hasty, acc
dental shot.

No point in taking chances.

Castillo looked through the study windows and saw n
one in the yard outside, but that meant nothing. For all b
knew, the sentries might have cooked up something in th
way of target practice to amuse themselves, but it wa
foolish of them not to warn him in advance.

If they were playing games, he meant to let them kno
that he wasn't amused. It was another question wheth
they would listen to him, but Castillo wouldn't let himse
be pushed around without a fight.

He tucked the Browning in his waistband, underneat
his sport coat, and was moving toward the study do
when he was shaken by the impact of a loud explosio
rippling through the house.

Castillo felt his lunch come back to haunt him an
fought down the sudden nausea with a determined force

ill. His enemies had found him somehow, and the sen-
ies were resisting. But who had come for him, and why?

New Amsterdam. It had to be. If his employers at the
GI had wanted to dispose of him, a phone call would
ave done the trick. Castillo's guards wouldn't resist an
·der from Havana. Rather, they would line up at his door
· carry out instructions from on high.

He had to get away. The guards might well be able to
rotect him, but he couldn't take the chance. Survival was
matter of preparedness and personal responsibility.

He left the study, closed the door behind him and
:aded toward the kitchen at the rear of the house. The
ack door was there and a garage with several cars inside.
·e had found by snooping that the keys were left in the
nition. Anyone who tried to stop him would be in for a
rprise.

Armand Castillo could depend on no one but himself.

HE TALLER of the sentries on the porch had glimpsed
ovement from the corner of his eye and glanced up in
me to see Encizo closing for the kill. It didn't save him,
; the subgun knocked him sprawling from his chair, but
's companion was a bit luckier, scooping up his rifle, fin-
:r on the trigger as he flung himself aside and out of
inge.

The first wild burst from the Kalashnikov came no-
here near Encizo. It was high and wide, perhaps an ac-
dental discharge, but it put an end to any hopes of taking
ieir intended target by surprise. Encizo only hoped that
olan had done better with the guards on his approach,
ducing the odds in the battle about to erupt.

The sentry came up firing, doing better this time, forc-
g Encizo to duck and cover, rolling to his left while bul-
ts chewed the lawn apart. It was too close for comfort,
nd the Phoenix Force warrior took no chances, palming
ne of the Russian frag grenades as he sprang to his feet,
inking the pin and unloading with an overhand pitch that
:opped the lethal egg dead center on the porch.

His target tried to scramble clear, but all in vain. T
blast punched him across the railing, tumbling his t
tered corpse across the lawn for several yards before
came to rest.

The door was clear so far. Encizo slung his subgun a
went to the Kalashnikov for greater stopping power, f
ing off a short burst through the door before he entere
It was cooler in the house, but that wouldn't last long.

He scanned the living room, saw no one and dropped
incendiary stick on the sofa before moving on. Son
where ahead of him, Armand Castillo would be waitin

The hunt was on, and Encizo wasn't about to quit t
fore he found his prey.

APPROACHING FROM THE EAST, or rear, side of the hou:
Mack Bolan heard the sound of rifle fire and knew t
stealthy approach was history. It would be fire and thu
der from that point on, and the sooner he could get insi
the house, the better.

He was racing off in that direction when a flicker at t
far periphery of vision stopped him short. A solitary fi
ure had left the house, running toward a large detach
garage several yards away. He couldn't see the runne
face, but he was decked out in civilian clothes, unlike t
sentries Bolan had disposed of.

Castillo?

There was only one way to find out.

He veered off course and headed in pursuit. The runn
had a strong lead and reached the garage in momen
pulled up the sliding door in front and ducked inside.
moment later Bolan heard an engine rev and a nonc
script sedan emerged, tires spinning in the gravel of t
driveway as it fought for traction.

The warrior moved to intercept the car, uncerta
whether he could stop it with his subgun but knowing
would have to try. The driver saw him coming, gaping
him through the windshield, and the Executioner ma

instant recognition of his target. Even with the fuzzy start of a mustache, there could be no mistake—Castillo.

The submachine gun stuttered, bullets knocking out one headlight and gouging the starboard fender. Castillo ducked behind the dash for cover, but he kept on coming, somehow holding fast on a collision course. He gunned the engine, rapidly accelerating.

Bolan had a choice to make. He fired a burst through the windshield, knowing it was wasted, then leaped aside to save himself. The black sedan roared past him, spitting gravel from beneath its tires, and the warrior came up firing from behind it, peppering the trunk.

Suppose he hit the fuel tank—would it matter? Lacking tracers or some other kind of spark, his rounds wouldn't ignite the fuel. Of course, Castillo might run dry a few miles down the road, be forced to walk a bit, but they could ill afford to stalk him on the highway.

He was going to escape.

The angry sound of a Kalashnikov distracted Bolan, drew his eyes back toward the house. He was in time to see Encizo step down from the porch and take a stance directly in the middle of the driveway, firing from the hip.

The Phoenix Force warrior didn't flinch as the sedan approached him, standing fast and emptying his magazine before he dropped the rifle, brought his subgun around and opened fire with that. Between the two guns—helped, perhaps, by Bolan's early fire—he blew the hood latch, and the hood flew open like the maw of a hungry alligator cruising for prey.

Only then, with smoke streaming out of the sedan's engine compartment, the vehicle swerving off course, did Encizo step clear. His subgun was empty, and he dropped it on the grass, drawing his Walther side arm as he followed the decelerating vehicle.

He was beside the car when it coasted to a stop, leaning in through the open driver's window with his pistol. Bolan didn't hear the shots, but he saw the Walther buck three times before it was withdrawn. Reloading where he stood, prepared for anything, he waited for Encizo to return.

"All done?" Bolan asked.

"Finally."

"We're finished, then."

He didn't have to add "For now." It was a given, in the sort of endless war they waged.

How long before another savage rose to meet them? How long would it be before their luck ran out?

Enough.

The evil of the day had been sufficient. They had both survived, their mission was complete, and second-guessing luck would always be a waste of time.

"They're waiting for us," Bolan said.

Encizo nodded, knowing he didn't refer to the Marines back at Guantánamo. "I'm done."

It was an object lesson for the enemy, and whether anyone would learn from it was questionable.

The Executioner could only teach. And hope.

Yes, there was always hope.

EPILOGUE

Election night.

The news came in to Stony Man by radio and television. The War Room held a modest crowd—Mack Bolan, Hal Brognola, Barbara Price, Aaron Kurtzman and Rafael Encizo. They had listened to returns throughout the evening off and on, although the outcome had been preordained.

Without Armand Castillo in the running, Martin Grandier was effectively unopposed. A hasty third-party effort had come to nothing, and late returns had Grandier sweeping into the prime minister's office by a landslide.

The investigation of Castillo's link with Medellín and the explosive violence of the week before the final vote was still continuing. Police had leaked substantial evidence connecting the absent former candidate with Colombian drug dealers, but there had been no suggestion as yet of a link with Havana.

Fair enough.

One brief report, sandwiched in between election returns, noted the arrest of a Grandier campaign volunteer, one Erno Soto, for his role in the kidnapping of Alicia Grandier. His confession was on record, but the men he named as masterminds behind the plot were all deceased—and violently, at that.

"I knew there had to be a mole," Encizo said.

"It stood to reason." Hal Brognola rose and stretched his arms above his head, joints cracking, before he moved to refill his coffee cup from the urn on a table nearby.

"Alicia gave him up, I understand," Bolan commented.

"That's the story," Brognola replied. "Seems like he jumped her at the campaign office and handed her off to Gutierrez. From there, I guess your pressure on the brothers got Francisco off the dime. He made Gutierrez an offer he couldn't refuse."

"That's it, then."

"For the moment," Barbara Price put in. "They'll have no end of problems cleaning up the mess Francisco and his brother left with the police and legislature in Hollandia."

"That's not our problem," Brognola told her. "Grandier's on top of it. If he needs help from DEA to get it done, they won't be holding back."

"The daughter's bearing up okay?" Kurtzman asked.

Encizo fielded that one. "She'll be fine. No major damage, after all."

"You got to her in time," Price added.

"I was thinking...." Encizo stopped short, a small grin playing at the corners of his mouth.

"Thinking what?" Bolan prompted, half sure of what was coming.

"That they might need help there for a while. The DGI might not give up as easily as the Colombians."

Brognola cleared his throat. "I take it that you're volunteering for a little overtime?"

"Well, if you think it might help..."

"I got a call from Grandier this afternoon," Brognola said. "He had the same idea... or maybe someone else suggested it."

Encizo colored slightly, but no one around the conference table risked a smile or joke at his expense. The Executioner wouldn't begrudge his friend a little working R & R.

The breaks were few and far between in Bolan's war, and Encizo had signed on to the end of the line. It was seldom enough that they made a clean sweep, let alone got any pleasure out of the experience.

If Encizo came up with a vacation in the process, who was harmed?

The war would be there waiting for him when he made it back to Stony Man. That much was guaranteed.

Take
4 explosive books
plus a
mystery bonus
FREE

Don't miss out on the action in these titles featuring
THE EXECUTIONER®, ABLE TEAM® and PHOENIX FORCE®!

The Terror Trilogy

Features Mack Bolan, along with ABLE TEAM and PHOENIX FORCE, as they battle neo-Nazis and Arab terrorists to prevent war in the Middle East.

The Executioner #61186	FIRE BURST	$3.50 U.S.	☐
		$3.99 CAN.	☐
The Executioner #61187	CLEANSING FLAME	$3.50 U.S.	☐
		$3.99 CAN.	☐
SuperBolan #61437	INFERNO	$4.99 U.S.	☐
		$5.50 CAN.	☐

The Executioner®

Nonstop action, as Mack Bolan represents ultimate justice, within or beyond the law.

#61184	DEATH WARRANT	$3.50	☐
#61185	SUDDEN FURY	$3.50	☐
#61188	WAR PAINT	$3.50 U.S.	☐
		$3.99 CAN.	☐
#61189	WELLFIRE	$3.50 U.S.	☐
		$3.99 CAN.	☐

(limited quantities available on certain titles)

TOTAL AMOUNT	$
POSTAGE & HANDLING	$
($1.00 for one book, 50¢ for each additional)	
APPLICABLE TAXES*	$_____
TOTAL PAYABLE	$_____
(check or money order—please do not send cash)	

To order, complete this form and send it, along with a check or money order for the total above, payable to Gold Eagle Books, to: **In the U.S.:** 3010 Walden Avenue, P.O. Box 9077, Buffalo, NY 14269-9077; **In Canada:** P.O. Box 636, Fort Erie, Ontario, L2A 5X3.

Name:_____

Address:_____ City:_____

State/Prov.:_____ Zip/Postal Code: _____

*New York residents remit applicable sales taxes.
Canadian residents remit applicable GST and provincial taxes.

GEBACK9